Born in Walsall of Indian and Welsh stock, and educated there and at Oxford, DAVID BAGCHI is an academic now based at the University of Hull. Starting out as a historical theologian he recently became, in what he describes as a shock career move, a theological historian. In 2010 he started pressing the wrong keys on his laptop, and two years later his first novel, a Tudor conspiracy thriller, won the TBS Novel Prize. The *Mystery of Briony Lodge* is his second work of fiction.

DAVID BAGCHI

The Mystery of Briony Lodge

BARBICAN PRESS

First published in Great Britain by Barbican Press in 2016
© David Bagchi 2016

We blithely acknowledge the living spirit of Jerome K.
Jerome & Arthur Conan Doyle, especially as imbued
in *Three Men in a Boat* & 'A Scandal in Bohemia'

Barbican Press, Hull and London
Registered office: 1 Ashenden Road, London E5 0DP
www.barbicanpress.com
@barbicanpress1

A CIP catalogue for this book is available from the British Library

ISBN: 978-1-909954-07-6

Typeset by Tetragon, London
Cover by Jason Anscomb of Rawshock Design

Printed and bound by Totem in Poland

To Fiona

'This book would not elevate a cow. I cannot conscientiously recommend it for any useful purposes whatsoever.'

—JEROME K. JEROME

'"It's quite exciting," said Sherlock Holmes, with a yawn.'

—ARTHUR CONAN DOYLE

Chapter One

Wednesday 12 June 1889

To Montmorency she is always *the* woman. The effect she had upon him, the day she intruded so bizarrely into our bachelor existence, was both instant and lasting. It happened in this way. Montmorency and I were discussing, in the civilized manner that only old friends can, the advantages to be gained from holidaying at home. Montmorency agreed with my every word. He really is the most intelligent soul I know.

At least, we were *attempting* to discuss this theme in a civilized way. There were four of us in the sitting-room, relaxing with our cigarettes after one of our landlady's better dinners—Montmorency, and George, and William Samuel Harris, and myself.

George and Harris kept interrupting with oafish ideas of their own, quite out of keeping with the elevated tone of our conversation.

'What we want is rest,' said Harris.

'No, we don't,' I said.

'Rest and a complete change,' said George.

'Nonsense,' I said definitively, reaching for another cigarette. 'We need stimulation. The daily round of labour, the routine of work, has dulled our senses.'

I spoke charitably, as befits a Christian gentleman, for Harris does no work of any discernible kind and George's wits were dulled long before he started in that bank of his. Indeed, I believe it is a requirement of his employment. Of the four of us, only Montmorency and I could justly be described as having useful occupations. My work is the writing of superbly-crafted historical novels, which have achieved no small success among a select, discerning readership. I refer of course to *The Perils of Hypatia*, a rollicking yarn set in fifth-century Alexandria, and *The Crucifer of Sidon: A Tale of the Crusades*. Montmorency, for his part, has an extensive practice which covers the entire neighbourhood, picking fights with opponents large and small. He more than earns his rations at home by terrorizing the rodent community of Baker Street, W1. Most have already packed their bags and gone. For all I know they have left warnings for any of their ilk who may wish to take their place, and penned furious letters to *The Times* about the appalling manners of the modern fox terrier.

'The quotidian diet of mere drudgery…' I continued, warming to my theme.

'Oh, do get on with it, J. You can be such a windbag at times.'

Ignoring Harris's ill-natured interruption, born of course of jealousy, I pressed on with my usual remorseless logic.

'Young men such as ourselves, with active minds (naturally I excuse you from this generalization, George) and active bodies (forgive me, Harris, I don't mean you, of course) do not need rest. Rest for us is the mere counterfeit of death. There will be time enough for rest when the Grim Reaper taps us on the shoulder and asks to see our ticket. No—what we need is *stimulus*, an opportunity to channel our boundless masculine energy into some new and unfamiliar direction. Just as when, in days of yore, a new-made knight was sent alone, unaided, into the furthest reaches of his liege-lord's kingdom, there to try his valour against all manner of foe and…'

'He wouldn't have been alone,' cut in Harris.

'What?' I asked, blankly.

'He wouldn't have been alone. Or unaided. He would have had a page. Someone to go before and announce him. Someone to carry his banner, so that people would say, "Oh look, there goes Sir Whatsisname".'

'All right,' I conceded grudgingly. 'He would have had a page. He would be sent alone, accompanied only by his loyal page, into the furthest…'

'Don't forget his squire,' Harris interrupted again. 'A knight must have a squire.'

'Isn't that the same thing as a page?' I inquired, less sure of myself now.

'"The same thing as a page"! Honestly, J., you seem to know remarkably little about history for someone who writes historical novels. Perhaps that's why no-one buys them. A squire is a knight's apprentice, a young gentleman who will grow up and be knighted himself. While he's learning the trade, he looks after the knight's armour. Gets out the old Brasso and polishes it up at the end of the day. You can't expect a knight to do that sort of thing for himself.'

'All right,' I said testily. 'The knight was sent alone, accompanied only by his loyal page and his trusty squire, into the…'

'You're forgetting the groom,' cut in Harris yet again. 'You can't have three horses and no-one to look after them.'

For a full half-minute, I did not speak. I could not trust myself to do so. Luckily for Harris, I possess a more-than-ordinary power over my base animal instincts. It was what saved his life that day. When at length I broke my silence, it was with a finely-judged admixture of dignity, ratiocination, and compassion for those who dwell on a lower intellectual plane than myself.

'The point I was making, Harris, was the general one that the young male of the species requires to be challenged. I was not discoursing upon the travelling habits of the medieval knight. Only a pedant of the most literal-minded stripe could possibly think I was.'

It was gratifying to see Montmorency announce his loyal support of my position by jumping up onto the window sill and barking at the street and wagging his tail in agreement. He goes through just the same ritual whenever a cab pulls up at the street door, but I suppose a fox terrier, lacking the power of speech (or so he says) has only a limited repertoire of signals with which to express his feelings. I thought it best to proceed to my conclusion as swiftly as possible, given that Harris was in a disputatious mood.

'But whereas many, including ourselves on past occasions, have sought adventure by travelling abroad, I maintain that in this great, brooding metropolis we call our home, there is to be found as much mystery, excitement, and romance as in the darkest souks of Maroc or the furthest pavilions of the Chinee.'

'Look, old man, if you're short of a bob or two for a trip abroad, you only have to ask: I'm sure George would lend you whatever you need.'

'No, Harris, I speak in earnest; yea, and never in greater earnest. Depend upon it: that our great mother-city of London longs to open up her treasure-chest of adventure to all her children. All she asks is that we agree to seize the very next opportunity that presents itself to us, without questioning or prevarication, without hesitation or procrastination. We must cast no backward glance, as did tragic Orpheus, nor turn again from the plough having once laid hand upon it. Provided one is open to all possibilities, adventure—blessed adventure—awaits.'

'What, in a dingy Second Floor Front in Baker Street?' asked George, who had been woken by Montmorency's barking. 'What adventure could possibly happen upon us here?'

At that precise moment, the Boots opened the door to my sitting room.

'Miss Briony Lodge,' he announced.

Chapter Two

---

*Of the power of female beauty upon the male brain—A
decorated ceiling—On the supernatural abilities of dogs—The
railway guide a threat to public morality—On the glorious
freedom of God's special creature, the locomotive—Harris has
an idea—The moral degeneracy of the downstream man*

As our fair visitor entered, we rose as one man.
Or, rather, as two men, for George had in the
meantime fallen asleep again and had to be roused
from his slumbers by a well-aimed cricket boot.

'Do come in, miss,' I said, hastily retrieving the
boot, which had bounced off George's forehead. No
harm had been done. The leather was quite undam-
aged, and the spikes had not been bent. George's
head, thankfully, had taken the brunt of the impact.

'And, pray, take a seat.' I indicated the chair
that George had so recently, and hurriedly, vacated.
'Harris, if you would be so good as to ring for tea.'
He did so, but with such a bad grace that he broke
the rope and had to go down and find Mrs Hudson
himself.

'Thank you, sir. And thank you, gentlemen, for permitting me to disturb you. I know that your time is precious, Mr Holmes, so let me come straight to the point. My name is Briony Lodge, and I am at present engaged as the acting-headmistress of a private girls' school in St John's Wood. Until three months ago I was the second mistress in a similar establishment in Walsall, run by Miss Violet Hunter.'

At this point I break from Miss Lodge's interesting narrative, not out of any disrespect to our visitor but in order to clarify a point for my readers which might otherwise be puzzling them. It must be remembered that, when a male of the red-blooded variety is involved, the proximity of a very pretty young woman—as Miss Lodge certainly was—is inversely proportional to his grasp of reality. Questions of right and wrong, truth and falsehood, even veracity and mendacity, become wholly subordinated to more material questions about the colour of her eyes (they were a deep, intense blue, verging on indigo), the shape of her nose (it had a noble, almost aquiline, sweep to it), and the curve of her lips (like a scarlet bow whose darts could pierce the hardest soul, if you must know). So when our beauteous visitor informed me that my name was 'Mr Holmes', it simply did not occur to me that she might be mistaken. After all, did not the ancient Greeks, who generally knew what they were on about, equate truth to beauty? In that case, how could any beautiful woman ever be wrong? (I know the answer to that one now. It is when you marry 'em. But at that stage of my life I was still ignorant of such deep matters.) Besides, I or she might have misheard, as the names 'Holmes' and 'Jerome' do very nearly rhyme. But let her resume her narrative.

'Miss Hunter recommended you to me as the only man in England who could shed light on my predicament. She told me that you had once helped her when she faced a not dissimilar dilemma. If you did not remember her name, she said, she felt sure you would remember her case, the affair of the Copper Beeches.'

'Yes, of course, the copper beaches. I remember them well,' I replied. (For an explanation of this temporary insanity, the reader is kindly referred back the space of two paragraphs. That will teach you to skip bits just because they look too long.)

'You must mean you remember *it* well—"The Copper Beeches" was a country house five miles from Winchester.'

'Of course—I remarked at the time that it was a singular name for a house lying so far from the sea.'

'Er, yes. Mr Holmes, perhaps I should proceed to the strange occurrences which have brought me here?'

Closing my hands together into an attitude of prayer, with my fingertips just touching my upper lip, in a gesture designed to convey both intense interest and wisdom beyond my years, I nodded sagely. That was a mistake. The combined effect of these two actions was that both index fingers became lodged in my nostrils. Luckily, our visitor was at that moment busy extracting a packet of letters from her bag, and did not notice my temporary predicament.

'You will see,' she explained as she untied the packet and passed it to me, 'that the first was dated a week ago and is postmarked from Oxford. The second, a day later, from Abingdon. The third, two days after that, is postmarked Wallingford. The fourth, dated the following day, is postmarked Goring and Streatly. The final one was sent the day after that, from Pangbourne.'

'That is really most interesting,' I said, managing to stifle a huge yawn so successfully that my pretty interlocutor could not have noticed it. 'But you seem to have neglected to bring the enclosures with you.'

'That is just it: there were no letters, no enclosures of any sort. Just empty envelopes. Oh!' she interrupted herself. 'Unless of course you count orange pips as an enclosure?'

'Orange pips? That is indeed most singular! Now, what fruit do we know of that has orange-coloured pips? A melon, perhaps.'

'No, Mr Holmes, you quite misunderstand me. The pips themselves are grey. They are from the fruit of an orange.'

'An orange. I see. No, Miss Lodge, there is no significance in that whatever. I conclude only that your correspondent is of a peculiarly tidy frame of mind and, being devoted to the eating of oranges, is constantly seeking receptacles in which to dispose of the pips. The envelopes he was writing to you merely served that purpose. I experience the same difficulty myself when eating olives: one never knows where to put the stones. But do go on with your interesting narrative. Do these envelopes yield any other clues?'

'No. As you can see, there is only the address, formed the same way on each envelope: "The Woman Briony Lodge, Serpentine Avenue, St John's Wood". It is a strange form of address.'

'It is,' I observed. 'They should of course have added "London" for the avoidance of any confusion.'

'I mean it seems strange to address me as "The Woman Briony Lodge". At first I thought it a deliberate discourtesy. But then it occurred to me that it might have been written by a foreigner, unfamiliar with our ways. But why would a foreigner write to me? Oh, Mr Holmes, what does this all mean? Is it merely a practical joke—perpetrated by one of my pupils, perhaps? Or should I worry that it is something more sinister? Whoever it is, for whatever purpose, they seem to be getting nearer to London by the day. I am at a loss to know what to do, which is why I applied immediately to my friend and mentor Miss Hunter, and why she suggested I come at once to 221b Baker Street.'

As she spoke, and as for the first time lines of worry sprang unbidden across her fair brow in the prettiest way imaginable, I realized that there was one point above all others I needed to settle at once.

'I can assure you, Miss Lodge, that you are in no danger. Nonetheless, it is an invariable principle with me to be prepared for any eventuality, no matter how remote. Tell me, do you have a sweetheart, a boyfriend, a fiancé, someone with whom there is an understanding of any sort, who might be able to offer you the manly arm of protection in case of need?'

'No, Mr Holmes. All my relatives live in Staffordshire. I have no-one in town. As for a fiancé, or male friends of any description—I scorn the very idea, for I am entirely devoted to my profession and to the young ladies in my care.'

Although I did my best to disguise it, I fear that Miss Lodge may have noticed that at this most welcome revelation I punched the air in the manner of a victorious gladiator. Fortunately, by the gift of quick-thinking, with which I have always been unfairly blessed, I was able to pretend that I was merely indicating a more than usually interesting patch of plasterwork above our heads. Miss Lodge followed my gaze, and uttered a gasp of shock.

'Goodness me—what on earth are they?' she cried.

For a moment I had no idea to what she might have been referring. And then I realized that she must have noticed the many bullet holes with which my ceiling was peppered. To the uninitiated, it must indeed have presented an alarming sight, but it was one to which I was now long inured.

'Oh, those. That is my downstairs neighbour, the First Floor Front. He occasionally takes pot-shots at his own ceiling with a revolver. He evidently does not realize that they pass through into my room, and hit my ceiling.'

'My goodness! He does this without warning? Is that not a cause for the greatest alarm!'

'Not at all. In fact, it works to my advantage. Mrs Hudson—my landlady, you know—is good enough to offer an appreciable reduction in my rent because of it.'

'A lower rent in return for the prospect of sudden death! It would alarm *me*, Mr Holmes!'

'Besides, Montmorency here always gives me a warning when the bullets are about to fly, and we go for a walk together. I don't know if he hears the rounds being loaded into the revolver, or whether he detects some subtle change in the mood of our downstairs neighbour such as invariably precedes his target-practice. I find it is best not to dwell too much on the praeternatural abilities of dogs: it puts me in a queer mood for the rest of the day.'

'If you are sure, Mr Holmes…' said our fair visitor, sounding not at all sure herself. 'But to return to the problem of the letters, and whether I should be alarmed about them or not: I wondered if my persecutor were travelling from Oxford to London by means of the railway.'

'It would have to be a very slow train, would it not, Miss Lodge? I mean, a day to get from Goring to Pangbourne. Mind you, I remember an awful journey I once had between…'

'I'm sorry to interrupt, Mr Holmes, but I fear you misunderstand me. I mean that my persecutor is perhaps following a railway route, taking the train between these towns and villages and putting up for a night or two at each, and posting these empty envelopes along the way.'

'Yes, that would make more sense. I see that. Yes, indeed.' I was conscious that I had no idea how to help this young woman, but I desperately wanted her to believe that I could. I decided to do the church steeple thing with my fingers again, except that this time I would refrain from excessively vigorous nodding.

'I suppose we would really need a railway timetable to establish whether this is a likely solution, would we not? Unfortunately, I do not have such a thing in my lodgings, nor in the school. We discourage the girls from using trains, you see, for fear of the adverse effects that high-velocity travel might have upon the developing female physiology. Do you perhaps have a Bradshaw here?'

At this point I should explain that I am a man of the most equable temperament. Not for me the old 'quick to anger' routine. Like the Stoic philosophers of old, I do not allow my fellow-man to give me the hump. I wish the Hyde Park Corner preachers a cheery 'Good day!' and pass on with a spring in my step. When I read the day's editorial in *The Times*, I merely respond with a phlegmatic 'Well, well—still, I suppose you have to earn your daily crust like the rest of us', and do not let it get me down. I move on. I regard with the utmost benignity the sound of the coalman making an early-morning delivery, and am hardly bothered at all by the sound of fingernails scraping blackboards. So it was not *my* reaction I feared at that moment. It was George's.

'A Bradshaw? A Bradshaw! Do *we* have a BRADSHAW?!' The effect was that of an approaching hurricane, meeting a couple of old friends of his, a tempest and a cyclone, on the way. 'If we had a Bradshaw,' said George, 'I tell you what I would do with it. I would take it round to old Bradshaw's place and beat him to a pulp with it. And then I would bury him. And then I would bury all the Bradshaw guides I could find with him. And I would dance upon his grave. And then I would sing a comic song on it.'

Luckily, George is very good at comic songs, so I imagine that would be some comfort for Mr Bradshaw's bereaved relatives in their time of grief.

'I don't think I understand,' confessed the beautiful Miss Lodge, prettily. 'How can you not like Bradshaws, Mr Wingrave?'

Her appeal was bootless, unlike George. He had found the other cricket boot and in an uncontrollable rage was belabouring himself about the head with it.

'My dear Miss Lodge, permit me to explain,' I interjected. 'We believe Mr Bradshaw's *Railway Guide* to be the joint editorial production of Messrs Satan, Lucifer, Beelzebub, Asmodeus, and the Antichrist combined. I strongly suspect that they set themselves up as a limited liability joint stock company with the express purpose of publishing it. You see, Bradshaw's *Guide* has the unfortunate effect of persuading people that trains run on time according to fixed routes. People believe it, and they are disappointed in those beliefs. They hope, and their hopes are dashed. They become angry. Worse, they become disillusioned. Until finally, worst of all, they are brought to abject despair. If they cannot believe their Bradshaw, they ask themselves, how then can they believe anything? The cold, comfortless wind of scepticism swirls about their hearts. Their faith in human nature is lost. Their faith in law, in politics, in religion—all disappears. And so the Devil's work is done.

'If only people would understand: the locomotive is a free spirit. It goes where it will, when it will. It cannot be constrained by timetables and schedules. Do not be misled by mere tonnage: a train may have the appearance of an overweight dinosaur; but it has the soul of a bird, nay, a butterfly, flitting from blossom to blossom as it listeth. One day it may wish to go to Swindon, another to Crewe. Or else, in its caprice, it might decide to while away the live-long day in the repair shed, and neither man nor beast can shift it. People wait for trains on platforms, and get angry when they are late. How foolish and how wrong they are! Rejoice rather that the locomotive exists at all, as one of God's freest and most unpredictable creatures, and give thanks that it thrives on liberty, while it is we mere mortals who are bound to run along the predetermined tracks of work and duty. How much better to turn up at a station, not to "catch" a train, as the vulgar expression has it, but rather to see if a train will settle upon the rails before you? It may well happen. If it does, by all means get on, but let it take you where *it* will, and when it will, in its sovereign freedom, and do not complain that it takes you to Edinburgh when you wanted Bristol, or that it gets you there five hours late. No—rather, rejoice. Again I say, rejoice!'

Just as I was waxing lyrical upon the subject, Harris entered with a tray of tea, and utterly spoilt the impact I knew that my oratory was making on Miss Lodge.

'Here's the tea. Mrs Hudson has gone out, so Boots and I had to shift for ourselves. Oh, that reminds me, Boots says you will need this.'

Harris removed a book from his coat pocket and laid it alongside the tea things.

'Apparently First Floor Front usually consults one at this stage in an interview with a beautiful visitor, he tells me.'

It was the latest edition of *Bradshaw's Railway Guide*.

'Perhaps I had better take that,' said our guest. 'I fear for Mr Holmes's blood pressure otherwise.' After a few moments she had found what she was looking for. 'Some of these stations are connected, but no railway connects Oxford with Abingdon or Wallingford,' she announced.

'What about the river?' asked Harris.

There are times when Harris amazes me with his insights. Of course, they are not, strictly speaking, his own insights. They are merely sparks that happen to fly off him when he comes into contact with my own, vastly superior, intellect, and which I permit him to pass off as his own original thoughts. It was I who was thinking about the river, but it was my mouthpiece Harris who gave voice to those thoughts. The old coves who used to look after the oracle at Delphi had a similar arrangement with the Pythia, I believe.

'I wondered how long it would take anyone to mention the river. You see, Miss Lodge, some months ago we took a trip up the Thames, Harris, Wingrave, Montmorency and I. And so we happen to know that all the places mentioned are on the river. Your persecutor clearly lacks moral fibre, and I believe we can say that he is no match for your new protectors, if you will allow us to be so named.'

'Of course. I am glad to hear that you wish to take on my case. But tell me, how do you know he is a man, and how can you deduce his moral character merely from his itinerary?'

'As to his sex, that is for the moment but a working hypothesis. My judgement of his character is, however, based on firmer evidence. First, we know from the direction of his journey that he is a downstream man. My colleagues here are all upstream men, men of might and courage who fight against the prevailing current in all matters, fluvial or otherwise.'

'But if his object is me, and I am in London, and he is starting from Oxford, what other direction could he take?'

'Please, Miss Lodge…' With a wave of the hand and a knowing half-chuckle, which reminded her firmly that I was the helper and she merely the helpee, I dismissed her train of thought. When women make sound points against you, it is sometimes best just to patronize them: that normally renders them speechless.

'Secondly,' I continued, 'it is quite evident from the nature of his communication with you that this man has more envelopes than writing paper—why else would he send you empty envelopes? Now, what does this immediately suggest to the observant mind? It suggests to me a man who writes many letters—perhaps letters of complaint to his grocer or to his bank, perhaps letters of disgusted indignation to the national press—and who consequently uses up much writing paper. But he still has envelopes aplenty because at the last moment his courage fails him and he tears his letters up! This is a man more lacking in gumption than in gum-arabic; who possesses not the courage of his own convictions; who is constitutionally incapable of seeing anything through to its conclusion. No, Miss Lodge, I deduce that you need have no fear of your epistolary persecutor.'

At this point, Montmorency, who from the moment of Miss Lodge's arrival had been staring at her in dumb admiration, punctuated from time to time only by the pitiful sighs and whimpers of one hopelessly in love, fell to barking. It was almost as if he were admonishing me, for having made a deeply foolish deduction in a matter that touched his beloved.

The following days would reveal how right Montmorency was.

Chapter Three

On knowledge, useful and superfluous—The unifying power
of ignorance—Blue eyes not admissible evidence in a court
of law—A visit from the constabulary—On the importance
of removing laundry tags—Montmorency sheds light

'RIGHTO, J.,' said Harris, indulging in his most vulgarian cant. 'Let me just get this straight. You've promised this female that you, me, and George…'

'Don't forget Montmorency.'

'… and Montmorency will protect her from person or persons unknown who may, or who may not, be sending her empty envelopes which may, or may not, be meant maliciously, while sailing, or rowing, or possibly swimming, down the Thames.'

'Yes, I have.'

'And in the process you have succeeded in falsely representing yourself as the foremost consulting detective in the land, whose name and features are known throughout the world.'

'No. That charge I absolutely deny. Her only

misapprehension was in confusing me with someone called Holmes, not this international detective-chappie of yours.'

'Exactly! She believes you to be Mr Sherlock Holmes, the greatest sleuth in the Kingdom, and for all I know the Empire too.' Harris stopped in full flow, and gave me the look he normally reserves for those occasional moments when my customary erudition escapes me. 'Good God, J.—you have no idea who Holmes is, have you?'

My editor (a sensitive soul who is of the unshakeable conviction that readers are people who go to bed at seven o'clock with a drink of warm milk, who do not swear even when they hit their thumb with a hammer, and who combine the intelligence of a gnat with the attention span of the average carp) has advised me that here I should explain how it is that a more than usually well-connected man-about-town such as myself could possibly have lived the better part of a quarter-century in London without encountering the name of Sherlock Holmes. The plain fact of the matter is that I had. I know not how. But if pressed to explain, I would ask to the reader to imagine a sort of valve, or gate, which controls, on a quite involuntary basis, the information which enters and leaves my consciousness. My brain, though more capacious than most men's (certainly than George's, though that is not to claim much), is of but finite capacity. Certain facts, which are important to me as a distinguished writer of historical fiction, such as the dates of St Cyril of Alexandria's birth and death, or the duration of the siege of Acre, are etched as deeply into the old cranium as the memory of my dear mother's face. But as I saw her only a week Sunday, that is not so surprising. Other facts, such as the bank rate, or the times of high tide in the Limehouse Basin, which I do not need to know, flow into my consciousness and out again. It is as simple as that: those facts which I need to know I store, file, and cross-reference. Those I do not need, such as the existence of an apparently brilliant but eccentric detective, I instantly forget.

If only others would follow my example. Half the misery in the world is caused by people hoarding facts that do not belong to them. When Mrs Choggins tells your wife that no. 21's second cousin saw you making love to the new barmaid down The Dog and Duck, it causes you no end of trouble. Yet what was that fact to Mrs Choggins? Nothing at all. It would have been better had she forgotten it instantly. At any rate, it would have been better for you.

Knowledge should be treated like lost property or stray letters. It should be returned to its rightful owner as soon as possible. No use should be made of it by those unauthorized. If necessary, it should remain in a secure location until called for. If only knowledge were less common, it would be more valued.

The concept of *general* knowledge I do not understand at all. If knowledge is generally known, what is the point of *my* knowing it? Why should I clutter up *my* brain with information already known to others? I could simply ask the nearest police-man whatever I wanted to know. (Though what we generally want to know is, where *is* the nearest policeman? In my experience, they are never to be found—when you want one. In my youth, when I often felt unequal to police company, they would appear in flocks of five or six together, all anxious to make my acquaintance and to inquire if I was enjoying being out in the fine night air.)

No—what the world needs is not general knowl-edge but *specialist* knowledge, so that each one of us has our own quantum of information vouchsafed to none other. This one would know how a steam engine works, but nothing else; that one would have binomial theorem tied up, but be unable to lace his boots; for that, he would have to apply to number three, who in turn would be quite ignorant of the Balkan question. And so it would go on. Then all distinctions of rank and birth, wealth and privilege, must fall away: each man, woman, and child would be precious and valued in the sight of all, for their unique knowledge, for the sum of humanity would depend upon its parts, the meanest as much as the noblest. Every family, tribe, nation, and empire would be forced to co-operate one with the other. There would be no more wars, for all must survive or none will. And at dinner parties, we would be able to say to our neighbour, 'Really? Do you know, I had no idea. How very fascinating.'

What is more, we would mean it.

And so it was, astounding as this might seem to his more fanatical followers, that I knew nothing of the identity and reputation of Sherlock Holmes, until that fateful day.

'Speaking as a lawyer, J. ...'

(So that is what Harris does for a living! I did wonder.)

'Speaking as a lawyer, J., I must advise you that you have put yourself in a most vulnerable position, all for a woman whose bona fides have yet to be established.'

'You did see her eyes, didn't you?' I said. 'Intensely blue, very nearly indigo.'

'I did, and I must further advise you that blue eyes do not constitute bona fides. Even if they are very nearly indigo.'

'Then there is only one thing for it. Montmorency and I will have to take a walk.'

At this, the said fox terrier leapt up onto the window sill once more and started barking and wagging his tail, showing his enthusiasm for the prospect of walking with me. It is also the routine he goes through whenever someone comes to the street door. But, as I have had occasion to remark before, the canine repertoire of communications is perforce a limited one, and the same gesture must do a double or even a triple duty.

'That lunatic First Floor Front isn't going to start shooting again, is he?' asked Harris, eyeing the carpet with suspicion.

'No. We are taking a walk to St John's Wood. Serpentine Avenue, I believe it was. I can at least establish that the address she gave was genuine.'

'How? You don't even know her house number.'

'There cannot be more than one, or at the most two, Briony Lodges in Serpentine Avenue, St John's Wood.'

'If you do find another, just send her to me,' piped up George.

'Do not be base and uncouth, George,' Harris and I said in unison.

Then Boots was at the door again, announcing another visitor.

'Inspector Lestrade of Scotland Yard,' the boy boomed self-importantly.

I nodded, settled back into my chair, and readied myself with my church-steeple finger pose. People whose views I respect in such matters have told me that it shows off my noble and superior profile to best advantage. Harris took up a position behind my chair, and from his hurried fidgeting I guessed he was adopting what he calls his 'l'Empereur' pose: one hand extended along the back of a chair, the other thrust Napoleon-style into his jacket. He looks quite ludicrous doing this, but he will brook no criticism. Some irresponsible halfwit once told him it makes him appear superior—noble, indeed. Harris is so easily flattered. George simply opened and closed his mouth repeatedly, like a fish, trying to say words that would not come: 'My God, it's the police!'

Lestrade was a man of commanding height and barrel-chested with it. His sunburnt face and close-cropped white hair gave him the appearance of a bronze statue in a pigeon-loft. He spoke with a familiar, thick, rather guttural accent that I could not for the moment place. He was accompanied by an equally imposing constable, a surly cuss who refused a seat when offered. My sitting-room suddenly seemed a much smaller place.

'Mr Jerome?' Lestrade asked.

'The same,' I replied, without rising.

'Mr Jerome Jerome?' he asked as he took his seat.

'The same.'

'Yes, I see it is the same again! You have the same name twice. Ha, ha, ha!' He cast around to his constable, who began laughing as heartily.

'Indeed,' I said coldly. 'To what do I owe the pleasure of your company, Inspector?'

'I understand that you were visited here this afternoon by a young woman by the name of Miss Briony Lodge. Is that so?'

'I can neither confirm nor deny it.'

The inspector suddenly looked flustered. 'But these informations I have from my constable received! It is impossible that he could be mistaken.'

'Inspector, would you kindly get to the point?'

'The point is that the woman who calls herself Briony Lodge is a confidence trickster. Oh, yes, we have known about this young lady for quite some time. She approaches young bachelor men, tells them some far-fetched tale about how she is being followed, or some such story, and that she needs their protection. Before they know it, they are lending her a large amount of money to leave the country, she makes her escape and is never seen again. Not by them, that is. She dyes her hair, changes her name, and moves on to her next mark. Quite a lucrative business.'

At this, Harris coughed significantly. His meaning was unmistakable: 'I told you so, you half-witted chump.'

George also began coughing. In his case, however, it signified only that he had snaffled a dry biscuit from the tray and found, too late, that there was no tea left to go with it.

'That changes things, Inspector. I must make a clean breast of it and apologize for not being frank with you from the start. The young lady you mentioned was here. And, yes, she did ask for my protection. I have no reason to believe that, in the fullness of time, she would not have unfolded the rest of her scheme in exactly the manner you describe.'

At this, Lestrade turned to his constable and uttered the single triumphant word, 'So!'

'So!' the constable agreed.

'Tell me, Mr Jerome,' Lestrade continued. 'What was the precise nature of the jeopardy that our Miss Lodge—as she calls herself—described to you? It is important that we know exactly what she said. Did she give you anything? Did she show you any letters, for instance?'

'Letters? No. She had no letters. What was it she said, Harris? Something about a one-eyed Chinaman with a peg leg, wasn't it? I remember that. How could one forget! And did he not have someone in tow with him? An Italian, wasn't it?'

'That's right, J. An Italian count with a duelling scar on his left cheek and a collection of specially trained white rabbits which never leaves his side.'

'As you can see, Inspector, it was a far-fetched tale she spun. And to think I was taken in by her!'

'Indeed,' replied Lestrade, thoughtfully. 'But she gave you no papers of any kind, nor showed any to you?'

'I'm afraid not. It may be that she was saving that little wrinkle up for a future visit.'

'Well, Mr Jerome—gentlemen—I see that our work here is done. But if she makes contact again, let me know at once. Do not try contacting me at the Yard. I am on surveillance at the moment and rarely at my desk. My card. I am at this address known.'

Lestrade stood up to go. As he did so, he said something which quite astonished us.

'You are fortunate, are you not, Mr Jerome, to have rooms above those of the celebrated detective Sherlock Holmes. He must be a most stimulating neighbour to have.'

'Sherlock Holmes is J.'s First Floor Front! How extraordinary—we were just speaking about him,' said Harris.

Lestrade muttered something under his breath to his constable about idiots, then made for the door. His constable hurried to open it. Was it the swiftness of the constable's movement that explains what happened next? I know not. Whatever the reason, the atavistic beast that lies within the soul of every fox terrier awoke in all its terrible fury, and Montmorency leaped at the constable, pulling at the sleeve of his jacket. For a moment the constable looked as if he would draw his truncheon and dash the little dog's brains out; but one glance at George, who had risen and was advancing rapidly towards him, made him think better of it, and an instant later both our visitors had shown themselves out.

'Well done, George,' I said.

'If he had touched Montmorency, I'd have swung for him, copper or not,' said George, who had evidently caught some of Harris's cockney cant. 'But what was all that nonsense you and Harris were spouting about Chinamen and Italian rabbits? I don't remember her saying anything about that. Mind you, I suppose I could have nodded off…'

'He's got a point, J., I played along with you, but what was that all about? It's a serious offence to lie to a police officer,' said Harris.

'It is also a serious offence to impersonate a police officer,' I responded, and waited to see the full effect of my revelation upon my interlocutors. 'How many Germans do you suppose Scotland Yard employs at the rank of inspector?'

'A German? Yes, of course, a German!' said George and Harris in unison.

Our jaunts through Germany had taught us one invaluable lesson, and that was how to recognize the common-or-garden male of the species.

'Was it the discourteous manner in which he treated his verbs that first put you on to him?' asked Harris.

'No. As a matter of fact I noticed it even before that—when he made a joke about my name. No Englishman would ever be so ungentlemanly as to make light of a person's name to his face. Behind his back, of course; but to his face, never. It is simply not done, and a genuine Scotland Yard officer would have known that.'

Montmorency—heroic Montmorency—put his paws upon my knee and looked deeply into my eyes. Dogs instinctively know when to give and when to withhold praise, the better to insure good behaviour in their humans. He was foaming a bit at the mouth, but I put this down to the excitement of the last few minutes.

'I've been thinking,' George admitted, bravely. 'Just because the man was a German does not mean he cannot be a real policeman—it's not cast-iron proof, I mean, is it?' It was a surprisingly good point, for George, and for a moment I was at a loss to answer him.

'What on earth has Montmorency got in his mouth?' exclaimed Harris.

'I don't know,' I said, realizing that what I had mistaken for canine spittle was in fact a white laundry tag between Montmorency's teeth. It was this he had been trying to show me, and this that he had wrested so tenaciously from the constable's sleeve. I took the tag. It read:

CUBITT & SON
Theatrical Costume Hire.

Underneath was typed the legend:

1 X POLICE (LGE).

A date by which the item had to be returned to the costumiers was written beneath that, in blue laundry marker.

'Well done, Montmorency!' we said in unison.

Chapter Four

Mrs Hudson's true reason for tolerating Holmes—On the dangers
of devoted Clio-worship—Mrs Hudson takes charge—We set
a trap—Observation of Mrs Hudson's methods profitable

'WELL, I can only say that I'm very sorry, gents: I was flustered and just on my way out, and must have told Boots to take the young miss to see the gentlemen in the Second Floor Front, when I meant the First. It's an easy mistake to make. Still, it worked out all right in the end, didn't it? I mean, the young miss got to see you, and you've taken up the cudgels on her behalf. Besides, Mr Holmes wasn't here to see her anyway—he's been out gallivanting all night in one of his disguises, I don't doubt.'

'But why did you never tell us that our down-stairs neighbour was Mr Holmes? Think of all the dollymops we might have impressed if we could have told them,' complained Harris.

'Yes, well, I don't know what sort of a house they keep where you live, Mr Harris, but I'll thank you not to use profundities under my roof. Besides, Mr Holmes is one of my best tenants, and I didn't want you bothering him with trifles—like getting him to find your dog when it runs off after a cat and gets lost. And don't say you wouldn't, because you would, wouldn't you?'

'One of your best tenants? One of your best tenants!' I repeated for effect. 'You do nothing but complain about him, Mrs Hudson: if he's not shooting holes in your ceiling he's messing with chemicals and making a vile stench all over the house. The other week I thought we must have had the drains up. But, no, it turns out it was your perfect tenant conducting an experiment with sulphur and ammonia.'

'Well, Mr J., you do have a point. I admit that Mr Holmes's behaviour can be a little erotic. But having him as a tenant means I get Dr Watson as a bonus, like. And when you get to my age, and when you're a martyr to various veins, like I hope none of you ever is, bringing a doctor round to the house gets expensive. And Dr Watson is always such a kind gentleman.'

'Ah!' I said. 'The truth at last!'

'Oh, no, Mr J., don't get me wrong. I like all my tenants. I was just as much protecting your interests, you know.'

'How is that, Mrs Hudson? Pray tell us,' I rejoined, sceptically.

'Well,' she said, hesitating just a moment longer than was comfortable for any of us. 'You're a famous writer, aren't you?'

'I have that honour.'

'And if Mr Holmes was introduced to you, he'd be up here every five minutes bothering you for facts about, that thing of yours, you know, the Crucible of Cider.'

'*The Crucifer of Sidon. A Tale of the Crusades*,' I corrected.

'That's the one. He'd go mad for that, would Mr Holmes. All knowledge is grist for his milk. He's a real polymorph. And not just you. Mr George is a banker. He'd be forever asking him about financial matters, reversible bonds and that sort of thing. And there's Mr Harris too. I'm sure he does something…'

'Actually, Mrs Hudson, I'm a solicitor,' said Harris proudly.

'There you are, see: that's a sort of a job, isn't it, dear? Mr Holmes would be forever coming to you and asking about contractive and tortuous law, and all that stuff. Your lives wouldn't be worth living once he got to know who you all were.'

Mrs Hudson was right, of course. Despite our youth, as a group of friends we have already made our mark in our chosen professions—some, naturally, more than others. I flatter myself, for instance, that I have the business of history pretty much sewn up. What I don't know about history is frankly not worth knowing. But there is, as my sage landlady indicated, a danger in celebrity. If it ever became common knowledge in the locality that this humble worshipper at the shrine of Clio dwelt in their midst, there would be a queue down to Marylebone Road and back. People would be continually asking me to settle arguments about who won what battle when and which king came first and whether Napoleon wore his hat like *that* or like *that*. Although Mrs Hudson can be very annoying at times, and although her choice of words can at times be inept, she is the salt of the earth, the strong rock on which Britain's greatness has been built. She is *considerate*—and of how many people can you say that nowadays?

'Yes, well, I'm glad that's settled. I'll leave you gents to work out how you are going to help Miss Briony.'

'Ah, there we have a difficulty, Mrs Hudson,' I said.

'How do you mean?' said our landlady.

'We've so little to go on,' explained George.

'Nonsense,' said Mrs Hudson brusquely. 'You're trying to get this mysterious letter-writer, or rather envelope-writer, before he gets to her, aren't you?'

'Yes,' I admitted, not quite knowing where Mrs Hudson's reasoning would take us.

'And you've also got this great hulking German, who calls himself Lestrade. He's a wolf in cheap clothing if ever there was, and he clearly means her no good either. So it's oblivious what you should do. Mr George, you should be protecting Miss Briony—no-one in their right mind would try anything with someone of your statue prowling about. The other two should be looking for this mysterious correspondent.'

'But where do we start?' Harris asked.

'Why, Mr Harris, that's simplicity itself! He's following an itinerant, isn't he? All you have to do is plot his process on a map, work out where he'll be when, and intercede him on the way.'

'But how do we do that?' I asked.

'If one of you gents was kind enough to allow me somewhere to sit… thank you. You, Mr George, go and find me a map of the Thames. And you, Mr Harris, go and find me a pair of dividers. And you, Mr J.'

'Yes?' I said expectantly.

'Do something useful and ask Maria to make us some tea. I'll have this wrapped up before bedtime.'

Mrs Hudson's way of getting something done is to get everyone else running about for her while she sits down shouting orders. I once had an uncle like her, Uncle Podger. But as his story is not very relevant I shall omit it for the sake of brevity.

When we were all seated around my dining table once more, our respective errands successfully completed, Mrs Hudson spread out the map and we pinned the corners down with the cruets. She used the dividers to estimate the average daily distance travelled by our antagonist, then fixed them at that measure to estimate his likely future rate of progress.

'Now this man, whoever he is, was in Oxford a week ago today. That's Thursday last week. Friday, he was in Abingdon, Sunday in Wallingford, Monday in Goring, and Tuesday in Pangbourne. He's taking 'is time, isn't he? Let me see: at that rate he'd have been in Reading Wednesday (Miss Lodge would've got the letter today, but after she left home in the morning.) So tonight he'll probably put up at Henley.'

Mrs Hudson was again right. For a downstream man he was making heavy weather of it. Either he was unfamiliar with the art of rowing, or he was aiming just to stay at the most comfortable hotels along the route. He sounded to me like the sort of man who would probably stay at Maidenhead.

'Then tomorrow he'll probably stay at Maiden-head,' said Mrs Hudson.

My contempt for the man was growing by the second. Maidenhead, as any upstream man will tell you, is the very negation of the spirit of the Thames. The Thames is a manly river for manly types. Father Thames can be a hard task-master; but he rewards hard work fairly, with aching muscles and a sense of achievement. When you have done a day's work on that river, you know about it, and you can pat yourself on the back (if your muscles allow you to move at all, that is) for having done it. But Maidenhead is not for the hard-working man. It is for the soft man to take his wife, or someone who can pass as his wife, for the weekend. One night, they should tow Maidenhead downriver and out into the North Sea, preferably in a Force Eight. Then the Maidenhead swell and his fair companion would know what the upstream man means by a dirty weekend.

'Saturday he'll be at Staines,' Mrs Hudson continued. 'Sunday Kingston, and on Monday he'll be knocking on a certain door in St John's Wood.'

'Then we shall set off for Maidenhead first thing,' I announced.

'First thing, Mr J.?', said Mrs Hudson. There was a distinct note of scepticism in her voice. For some reason, she did not have me marked down as an early riser.

'On the dot, Mrs H.', I replied resolutely.

'Well, they do say that punctuation is the politeness of kings. But let me play the Devil's avocado for a moment. Suppose you do meet this man, the letter-writer, in Maidenhead: how would you know what he looks like?'

Mrs Hudson, once again, had a point.

'Then what should we do?'

'That's easy. At crack of dawn, Mr Harris should go to Goring and Streatly, and you to Pangbourne. You should both ask about all the strangers who were there on Monday or Tuesday, whichever—and especially any who visited the local post office to send any letters to London. Make a careful note of all the descriptions you are given and any names, and *then* meet at Maidenhead and swap notes. By a process of illumination, whoever is on both your lists must be a suspect. With any luck, you'll be able to track him down in his hotel that night, and tell him his little game is up. Otherwise, you go on to Staines the next morning, and wait to see who shows up there.'

For a moment, there was silence. All of us simply stared at Mrs Hudson. We saw in her eyes the gleam, the intensity, as she plotted the ambush of our human quarry. And in that moment we four were transported by some magic of common humanity back, back, back to the twilight of the primeval forest, where our Neanderthal ancestors, gathered in the flickering light of the camp fire, shared their tales of the chase or laid out stratagems for the morrow's hunt, in grunts and groans too deep for words. For all our trappings of civilization, for all our technology—the tram, the steam engine, the electrical hot-iron—it takes but little to reduce us to our primitive state even now. 'Reduce', I say; but who among us can claim that our existence then was not more honest, more noble, more uncluttered? And who truly would prefer our 'modern' life—a life of artifice, of pretence, of unnecessary lumber? No—give me the forest, the stout bow, the straight arrow, the fellowship of the chase, and the primordial grunting of the primitive Neanderthal.

'Or we could just go to Reading,' said Harris.

'How do you mean, Mr Harris?' Mrs Hudson asked.

'Well, he was there more recently than he was at either Goring or Pangbourne, and people's memories of him will be fresher.'

'That's not a bad idea, Mr Harris, but I think you'll find that my suggestion has certain advantages over it. A stranger is more likely to be noticed in a small, quiet place than a large, busy one. Besides, you could go round all the hotels and guest houses in both Goring and Streatly in a morning. In Reading, it would take you a week, and you still couldn't be sure you'd seen them all.'

'That's true,' we said in unison.

'But Mrs Hudson, it is as if you have thought this all through in advance. Your powers of analysis and strategy amaze me,' I added.

'Oh, Mr J.: such flatulence! You are very kind; but it all comes quite easy to me. I'm a landlady, you see. A landlady has to have good powers of observation, to see whether the slavey is drawing off liquor from the descanters. You've also got to be a good student of human caricature, else how could you choose a lodger who won't do a moonlight flit or murder you in your bed? Then there's the whole business of planning ahead, making sure we don't run out of your Gentleman's Relish, Mr J., and that there's enough cold Bass in for when Mr Harris comes calling. Compared with all that, your little problem doesn't seem all that untractionable. I know it's a fault with me to be too self-defecating. But on this occasion, gentlemen, I dare say you won't go far wrong if you observe my methods and apply them. Mr Holmes always does.'

Chapter 5

*The problem of male clothing—The proper nourishment
of the inner man—Harris revealed as a snail—
The impudence of Wiggins's boys—The London cab
not bound by laws of physics—On the importance
of parents' being truthful with their children*

WE retired that night, filled with delicious anticipation of the adventure to come. Our plans for the morrow were complete. After breakfast, George would go to St John's Wood, there to find the house of our beautiful client, and to establish himself as the last line of defence against the enemy. He would be, as it were, the goalkeeper. But to Harris and me fell the more responsible task of centre-backs. We it would be who would seek out and run down our enemy. By our watchfulness in defence, by our fleet-footedness in interception, by our ruthlessness in the tackle, and by our creative flair once the initiative was ours, we would turn defence into attack with a speed and panache that would leave our opponents reeling.

But first there was the problem of what to wear.

For fashionable Maidenhead, I should need my best boating costume. I could be sure that no-one would so much as speak to me, let alone consent to be interrogated as to the movement of suspicious boaters, unless I were dressed like a river swell—the sort that goes nowhere near the water except to be photographed. So I got out my boating set and laid it out carefully on the bed. I knew from experience that careful preparation in the laying-out of one's things in the correct order is the surest guarantee of swift and efficient packing.

But Maidenhead was not my initial destination. Pangbourne was. And to insinuate myself among the honest riparian workers there my boating costume would be more hindrance than help. It would mark me out as a fancy-dress man, not to be taken seriously; as one to whom work—real manly work like fishing, chandlering, lock-keeping, weir-maintenance, and driving notices into the riverbed which say 'Keep Out' and 'Private'—is alien. No—for that phase of my investigation I should need my fishing clothes and my fishing gear. These too I laid out carefully on the bed.

Neither of these costumes, it occurred to me, would do for travelling on the fast train to Reading, or even for going round the hotels and guest houses.

One set was too theatrical, the other too workman-like. And so I got out my travelling clothes and laid them carefully out on the bed with the others.

Then came the question of how long we would be away and how many shirts and sets of under-garments I should need. We did not know when we could return to our lodgings, so it was best to err on the side of over-provision. All these I set out on the bed with my now customary care. Also, it being July, the weather on the river was bound to be changeable. Both winter warms and waterproofs would be needed, and these too were now laid out on the bed.

I could no longer see the bed.

In retrospect, perhaps I had been too unselective, and perhaps some reconsideration of my travelling wardrobe was indicated. But, in spite of my growing weariness—it had been a long and eventful day—I felt a more urgent need now pressing upon my consciousness. For what Thames-man worth his salt would venture forth without reserves of sustenance? Not, of course, for the base purpose of satisfying the mere appetite of our stomachs. Far from it! Our greatest weapon in the coming battle would be our brains. Our enemy had already shown himself to be both resourceful and cunning, and to overcome him our grey matter would have to be in pretty much tip-top condition. The mind cannot work long at that level of intensity without food. I therefore resolved to go down to the pantry and select a few morsels—the barest minimum that would not add greatly to my burden but which would provide the exact nourishment my brain would need. But as I have often been told that my cranium is significantly larger than other men's, a sign surely of a larger than average brain, it would be foolish to stint on this aspect of my preparations. And so, when the house fell quiet, I left my rooms and descended stealthily to the kitchen.

Luckily, the pantry was equipped with just the resources I needed. My eye was first caught by a large pork pie, which I bagged immediately. Alongside this was a meat pie, which surely no-one would miss. Ha! And there was one of Mrs Hudson's large fruit pies—my brain never felt more refreshed and ready to take on the world than when I had just eaten a slice or two of a Mrs Hudson special. For a moment it did occur to me to take a knife to these items and remove just what I needed and no more. But I quickly decided, and surely rightly, that they would be far easier to transport in their entire state: they would be less messy (especially the fruit pie), and keep their freshness longer. Adding a few other necessaries on my way out—a smaller pork pie in case the first were insufficient, a second fruit pie, a few bottles of beer, some fresh fruit, and a tin of pineapple, to which I am especially partial—I returned to my rooms with the stealth with which I left. Harris could bring his own food, I thought uncharitably.

It had been a very long day, and it was now well into the night. We would need to rise before dawn to get to Pangbourne and Goring as early as possible, and sleep was of the highest priority. On reaching my bedroom, weighed down by tiredness, I dragged myself to the bed, swept the clutter of clothes straight on to the floor, fell onto the pillow and was instantly asleep.

*   *   *

Thursday 13 June

The following dawn found us shivering on the pavement outside Mrs Hudson's. Harris went off to get a cab, leaving me with the baggage. There seemed to be somehow far too much of it, considering that it was just two of us going away overnight. Unlike me, Harris does not know the meaning of travelling light. He is of the snail mentality, which is to say that he is truly happy only if he can bring his entire household, contents and all, with him. I, on the other hand, am of the avian persuasion: all I need is myself, and I am ready to fly. What care I for clothing or for food? Such trifles can be ignored. Virtue is the proper clothing of man, and honesty his meat and drink. This is something that Harris will never learn.

Harris's baggage taking up almost the full width of the pavement, and a good deal of the frontage of the house, it was not long before it had attracted a small crowd. Chief among them was a group of street arabs whom I had seen many times in Mrs Hudson's house, running up and down the stairs to the First Floor Front, which we now knew to be Holmes's rooms. It seemed that he employed them on detective errands from time to time, and they would often pay speculative visits to Baker Street on the off-chance of employment. Today, unfortunately, was one such day. Their leader was a boy called Wiggins, who was never to be seen but mounted upon some bicycle he had managed to obtain. Today it was a velocipede.

'What is it, mate? You openin' up an old clothes' stall on the pavement? You'll 'ave the rozzers on to ya if you do!' called out one of Wiggins's boys.

'Looks more like a food shop,' another shouted. 'Have you seen the size of that pork pie? It would feed our lot for a month.'

'Nah, can't you see 'e's off on an hexpedition? Going to find the source of the Hamazon I should think, and then visit the Niagara Falls on 'is way 'ome—why else would he want waterproofs in July?' Wiggins himself added, to general amusement.

I stood in martyred silence, wishing that Harris would hurry back with the cab. When he did, the cabman offered to take only half of the baggage, as he feared for the integrity of his axle if he took more. It turned out, however, that the axle's load-bearing capacity was, by some quirk of mechanical engineering unique to the London hansom cab, directly proportional to the size of the tip offered. And so I, Harris, and all Harris's luggage, set off for Paddington Station.

*　　*　　*

Having found three porters willing to carry our cases to the concourse and having bought our tickets, Harris and I took a vacant bench from where we could see the departure notices and the poor members of the public who were taken in by them.

'Oh, look, Harry,' said one woman. 'Here's the train for Bristol. Platform Three. It's leaving in ten minutes. Let's get on.'

Harris and I exchanged glances. The words, 'What a sad, deluded pair they are' did not need to be uttered.

A few seconds later a family group came along. 'Now listen carefully, children. Your Papa has just gone to buy the tickets, and we'll be leaving for Paignton in half-an-hour. So be sure you all stay together and no-one is to wander off. Do you hear me?'

The poor tribe, we thought to ourselves: how very irresponsible for a mother to bring up her children to believe in such stories.

In the meantime our attention had been drawn to a likely-looking engine on Platform Six. There was no destination displayed, but the engine looked healthy and willing, and we thought it might be persuaded to take us to Reading, if treated gently and with respect. We told the porters to stand by with our cases and await our instructions, but on no account to come near the train until we signalled. Then we sauntered down the platform towards the pulling engine with no more apparent purpose than if we were taking the air on Margate promenade.

'That is a fine-looking engine,' I called up to the driver. 'Do you suppose it might want to go for a run today?'

'Well, that I don't rightly know, sir,' replied the driver, intending like me to be overheard. 'He had a run only yesterday, as far as Oxford and back, so I don't suppose he'll be interested in going out again this week. Look at the pressure-gauge: there's hardly enough steam there to blow the whistle, let alone pull all these carriages. Perhaps if you and the other gentleman were to come back this time next week, he might be more in the mood.'

'That is a shame,' said Harris. 'Such a fine-looking engine too. I felt sure that a handsome specimen like this one would be able to go as far as, say, Reading, at high speed. But then you can't always tell by appearances, can you? Perhaps he was the runt of the litter and doesn't have the stamina of his brothers and sisters. He is obviously more suited to local work only, and shunting empty wagons.'

All the time Harris was speaking, the engine's boiler was stirring into life.

'That's often the case,' I shouted over the increasing din. 'Now I can see him more closely, though, it is obvious that he lacks the structural strength and boiler capacity of a *real* engine. He could never pull that many carriages.' At this point the engine's whistle blew hard. The driver winked at us and signalled the fireman to start loading the furnace. 'And certainly not as far as Reading—let's face it, he's no Express, is he?' We both laughed and shook our heads at the very notion.

The whistle blew again and the fireman continued shovelling. The driver checked the pressure-gauge and whispered conspiratorially to us. 'I'd get on board quickly, gentlemen. I reckon he's about ready to leave now.'

We beckoned the porters to come at once, and the last parcel was thrust through a window just as the train was moving off. In the distance, we could see the couple for Bristol and the family for Paignton walk away from the departure boards, dejected looking.

And that is how Harris and I persuaded the stopping service to Gerrard's Cross to become the Plymouth Express.

Chapter Six

---

*George rises early—converses at length with a total
stranger—earns seven years' bad luck—encounters a
vision of loveliness and has an unworthy thought—
commits arson—ponders much upon tricky questions*

ALMOST immediately after our departure from
Paddington—or within a couple of hours, at
most—George began to stir from his bed. Soon—or
within a couple more hours, at most—he was on
his way to St John's Wood.

It appears that Serpentine Avenue was named,
not after the lake, but on account of its meandering
course. One end of the street cannot be seen from
the other, and the middle stretch is quite invisible
to both ends. George turned into it and almost
immediately spotted someone coming the other way.

'Briony Lodge?' asked George.

'Round the bend on your left, mate.'

'Thanks.'

'Don't mention it. Mind you, looks like a bit of
a ruck kicking off round there.'

'Oh… righto.'

There really is no stopping George on a subject, once he has got started.

Soon he was at the place indicated by the stranger, where a singular sight greeted him. For in this quiet suburban street, which would normally be deserted at this—or any other—time of day, a veritable crowd had gathered: several young swells, a group of roughs, two guardsmen and a nurse, an itinerant knife-sharpener, and a non-conformist clergyman. A fracas had indeed broken out—something to do with a lady's carriage that had just arrived at the house—and the clergyman was remonstrating with the roughs. George saw the danger and, fearless of any harm to himself, waded in. That is George in a nutshell (though the notion of squeezing George, who weighs about twelve stone, into a nutshell is difficult to grasp). Going up to the rough who had the clergyman by his lapels, George wound himself up to strike the hardest blow he had ever landed upon another man. Sadly, his aim was not equal to his vast strength: he laid the clergyman out cold on the pavement. The lady—not Miss Lodge—who had just arrived stood on the steps of her villa and called out, 'Oi there—how's the old cove?' (Or something to that effect: bear in mind that I was told of these events in George's words).

Some people in the crowd cried out that the poor man was dead. George took this hard. He had heard somewhere that killing a clergyman, even accidentally, brought seven years' bad luck. But then George saw the poor man's eyes flicker open, so he cried out, 'No—he's alive. Reckon he's none too chipper, though.'

'Bring him in here, and someone send for a doctor,' called out the lady.

George picked up the cleric and started for the villa's front door. But as he passed the gatepost he saw something that made his blood run cold. Inscribed into the stone, in clear roman letters, were two words: 'Briony Lodge'. He realized instantly that this was the name of the villa, not of its inhabitant. He was confused; but fate had handed him a passport, in the unlikely form of an insensate clergyman, into the villa where his myriad of questions might perhaps be answered.

The butler showed George and his burden into the sitting room, where the lady was waiting, and for the first time George could take in the vision of loveliness that stood, wringing her hands in anxious care, before him. Where Miss Lodge was pretty in a provincial way, the mistress of this house was stunning in every way. Hers was a face that a man might die for, said George, who is not usually given to poetic expression of any sort. Apart from singing comic songs, of course.

'Put him here on the sofa,' she said. 'It is very comfortable.'

George did so, and observed the exquisite kindliness with which she attended to the elderly gentleman. The ignoble thought stirred in his breast, that it would be worth a man's getting knocked down outside this lady's house a few times, if it meant being cared for by such an angelic creature. At length she stood and drew herself up to her full, majestic height. She addressed George directly.

'You have been very kind, sir, in helping this poor man. I wonder—may I presume upon your kindness for a few moments longer? I need to give instructions to my servants and get a few things to help this minister to be more comfortable. More importantly, I want to check for myself that a proper medical man has been sent for. If not, I shall summon my own physician. Would you kindly wait here until I return to relieve you? Stay with our guest and reassure him, if he asks, that he is safe and among friends. Would you do that for me? My name, by the way, is Irene Adler—or rather Mrs Godfrey Norton, as I am now.'

Her voice had the deep, seductive quality of a contralto. Her modulation was finer than that of any trained actress. By her word alone, she had the power to send any man to face certain death, if that were her command. But, coming as it did from those lips, that face—George had no say in the matter. He could but mutter his own name in return and nod his assent.

Left alone, George first checked that the recumbent incumbent was still in the land of the living. He was, and what is more a beatific smile seemed to play upon his lips, as if he were thinking pleasant thoughts. George calculated that he would probably suffer no more than two or three years' bad luck for this, or there was no justice in the world. Less, if the clergyman made a full recovery.

More settled in his mind, he decided to see what entertainment the rest of the sitting room could offer him. Decanters there were none. But he noticed a gas lighter, and decided to smoke one of his obnoxious cheroots while waiting for the lady of the house to return, and while he put his mind—what there was of it—to the mystery of Briony Lodge. First, is she a woman or a house? She claimed to be a woman, but he had only her word for that. On the other hand, the gatepost of this villa provided solid proof that Briony Lodge, Serpentine Avenue, was a house, and a substantial one at that. The girl was lying! Secondly, for what purpose had she lied? He could not tell, but he knew only too well the result: her lie had sent his friends J. and Harris to the banks of the Thames, to face who knew what danger. Thirdly, what did the mysterious policemen signify? Perhaps nothing but to lend credence, and a vague sense of peril and urgency, to her story.

To dispel, as far as possible, the foul stench of the cheroot (it must be remembered that he was smoking in another's house without permission, and that guilt can stir, from time to time, even in the breast of an insensitive oaf like George), he opened the long windows that gave out onto the front lawn. While doing so, he inadvertently caught the curtain with the lit end of his diabolical cigar, and soon the smoke was rising cheerfully into the sitting-room. George, already feeling guilty, was worried that he might be blamed for burning down the well-set suburban villa, and decided to make his move, and escape while he could. He felt bad about leaving the semi-conscious clergyman to burn to death—which just shows that even George has his good points—and so, before leaving via the same window, he called out in a voice loud enough to wake the dead, 'Fire! Fire!'. As he left, he heard the assembled crowd outside return the shout. Safe in the knowledge that the alarm had been raised, he made his way surreptitiously round the back of the house, and left the scene via Serpentine Mews. His one thought was to return to Baker Street and alert his comrades to the new and surprising turn that events had taken.

Chapter Seven

The Eastwall Hotel,
Oxford,
Thursday 5th June

MY dear Holmes,
The best possible news—I have him! From the excellent photographs supplied by your brother Mycroft, and with the co-operation of the Oxford City Police, it was only a matter of time before I tracked down the one known as 'Jan'. You asked me to provide you with the fullest possible details of everything connected with this fiendish conspiracy, and to dismiss no fact, however apparently small or insignificant, as unworthy of your attention. What follows, therefore is the full story of our Bohemian friend's interception.

The city of Oxford is so designed—or rather, has over the years so developed in its charmingly higgledy-piggledy way—that any visitor who spends more than a few hours there must sooner or later traverse the central crossroads, its *carrefour*, as the French would have it, known here as Carfax. There is, therefore, no need actively to seek out anyone in Oxford, a fact which seems to suit the sedentary and studious nature of its scholarly inhabitants: wait at Carfax long enough and the one you seek will come to you. And so it has proved, my dear Holmes! This morning I was standing by the railings outside Carfax Church, watchful behind my newspaper, when one of the policemen regularly stationed there (but who like the other constables had been shown the photographs) beckoned discreetly to me and drew to my attention a strangely-garbed fellow walking towards the High Street from the west. This was not long after the church clock above me had chimed eleven.

Despite his highly theatrical oversized cloak and broad-brimmed hat which obscured half his face, I saw enough of him to be able to second the constable's identification. I waited awhile before setting off, for I decided to follow him at a considerable distance. I was rashly confident that such a costume would make him easily distinguishable for miles, while I would be in no danger whatever of being seen by him, still less identified as a pursuer. And it is true that in any other provincial town or city in England, such a 'disguise' would have been quite useless—the more so at the height of summer—in that it would unfailingly have drawn far more attention towards him than it could possibly deflect. In Oxford, however, as I was soon to discover, almost at great cost, matters were arranged quite differently.

It was as he approached Magdalen College that I realized my mistake. For there, spilling out of the porter's lodge to fill the pavement and even some of the road, was a veritable sea of Magdalen men of the 'Lord Alfred Douglas' type, all dressed in flamboyant fashion completed in every case by a swirling black cloak and broad-brimmed hat. Jan was soon absorbed into this throng, a drop of black in an ocean of blackness. I looked on in horror as this party made its way across the road towards the University's Botanical Gardens. I would have to follow, but what chance had I of finding my man amongst them?

A fracas was evidently developing at the splendid gates to the Botanic Garden, and I hastened my pace to catch up. As I approached, the reason became obvious. The keepers of the Gardens meant to deny access to these flamboyant undergraduates, and were not only remonstrating with very direct language, but were also wielding hoes and grass-scythes in an intimidating manner. I know that many feel threatened by the outward display of aestheticism in their fellow men, and I appreciate that such feelings would be magnified in the presence of such a large concentration of Magdaleners. However, whatever one's personal prejudices about such matters, to me it seemed insupportable to use that as a reason for depriving anyone of the simple enjoyment of nature, and I determined to uphold the rights of the black-cloaked multitude. Although my own position was weak—being neither a current nor an old member of this ancient university, nor even a citizen of Oxford—I headed directly for the leader of the keepers in order to give him the benefit of my opinion on the matter. I need not have concerned myself: the press of Magdaleners was so great that the garden-keepers were simply trampled underfoot by them. After making sure that all of the keepers were still alive and likely to remain so, I followed the mob into the gardens proper. There I witnessed the reason for the gardeners' reluctance to admit these men. It was not, I now realized, borne of unthinking prejudice, but of an understandable professional desire to prevent the fruit of their labours from being consumed. For each undergraduate, ignoring the clearly-printed signs, which populated the gardens quite as abundantly as the plantings, forbidding just such actions, now cut for himself a colourful buttonhole from the flowers on display. The more exotically-minded members of the throng made for the hothouse, no doubt with the same end in view. The search for fresh blooms was evidently a daily occurrence, and at this rate of consumption the University's flora could surely not stand another two days' such depredation.

As each man gathered his bloom, he stood aside to let another black locust take his place, until each was newly decorated with a fresh flower representing the full gamut of the spectrum and more besides. All except for one man, whose pathetic return was a simple daisy, plucked from a wheelbarrow of mown grass, and a none-too-fresh one at that. In such a company, a man who was not a true aesthete, but only feigning aestheticism in order to avoid detection, stood out, despite his cloak and hat. I had regained contact with Jan, and I would not lose him again.

I observed him take lunch at a café near to the Queen's College, then in the afternoon followed him down to a boat-hire firm on the Isis, where I overheard him book a single-sculled boat for 9 a.m. the next day. I quickly booked a similar craft myself for 9.15, then followed him back up St Aldate's to the General Post Office. I followed your advice and kept to the other side of the road and observed him as much as possible in the reflections of shop-fronts. I witnessed him place an envelope in the posting box, outside the post office, marked 'London & the Home Counties'. Was it addressed to the lady in question? I know it is wrong to speculate in the absence of sufficient data, but it seems, as you yourself suggested, that he may be trying to intimidate her so that she acts precipitately in the matter of the photographs, to the inevitable discomfiture of our ~~royal~~ noble client.

So tomorrow morning will see me on the river, for the first time since my varsity days in London. I shall follow my prey and report by letter as I am able.

Chapter Eight

On the extraordinary effects of country air—The guile
of the seasoned huntsman—On the extraordinary
effects of country air (again)—The guile of the
hunted—My long-lost Uncle Toby found

Thursday 13 June

AT Reading, Harris and I decided to stow
the bulk of our things at left-luggage, to be
retrieved later. We then boarded the slow train
to Oxford. I dismounted at the very next stop,
Pangbourne, and waved Harris off on his way to
Goring.

Pangbourne, by common consent, lies on one
of the loveliest stretches of the Thames. For the
city-dweller, however, the prospects hereabout offer
something far more profound than picture-postcard
prettiness. They offer *refreshment*, and I do not mean
that sticky concoction they mix with water and try
to sell you for thrupence a throw, if you are fool

enough to buy it. No, I mean the soul's refreshment which our universal mother, the Lady Nature, wishes to bestow upon all her offspring. For what denizen of the city does not feel his heart thrill within him when he is once enfolded in nature's verdure? The grey city, which we falsely call our 'metropolis', is no true mother to us. For her we slave; and each day spent upon her streets and in her tenements we grow meaner and baser, for we grow further from our roots. And yet: and yet we know we are of noble stock, queen-born, and we long to find our true, royal mother.

Come to me, she seems to call, and rest awhile your weary head upon my breast. City worker and merchant, shopboy and shopgirl, clerk and man of accounts, drayman and coster: cast off your heavy garb of care, lay down your burden of worry. Let them slip away betimes, to fall into my deep currents and thence be swept out to the tide beyond, where waves of Sorrow must break, ere long, upon the shores of Joy. Fill your hearts, my children, with such clamour as I provide: the distant rasp of grasshopper; the song of gentle thrush; the cheerful hubbub of the bee, who for his honest toil wins sweeter reward than thy slave-wage. Nay, listen with yet more profit to my silence: the swan upon the water; the swallow upon the wing; the growing of the flower and the leaf. In my deep silence, let your strength return, let your thoughts be purified, let your lips breathe only my sweet breath. Until at length, as if born from me again, you return to the noisy city, there again to be sullied withal, yet never forgetting your mother's embrace.

It was not yet 9 a.m. when I stepped out into the station road and filled my lungs with good Berkshire air. I felt the inner transformation begin. Simply by breathing in this rich atmosphere, and exhaling the miasma of London from my body, I was sloughing off the city and reverting—or perhaps evolving—into a different creature: the countryman. It is always there, deep in the inmost recesses of every Englishman—his country self. Nobler, freer, stronger than his city soul, bound as the latter must be by the craven limitations of urban life. My senses were instantly more potent. Contours were sharper to my eye, colours more vivid. Sounds which with mere city-ears I could never have heard now came to me through the clear air with the pellucid clarity of a churchyard bell. It was as if Nature herself were endowing me with her panoply of arms, equipping me to track down my quarry in a righteous cause. Even my sense of direction was miraculously more acute, more sure. I set off resolutely, every nerve steeled to the coming chase.

'You be going the wrong way, sir.'

'What?' I said, spinning round to see the station-master leaning out of his office window.

'That's the wrong way. I assume you'll be wanting the river, what with all that fishing gear you've brought with you.'

'Er… yes,' I said. My ensemble of waterproofs, waders, rod, spare line, spare waders, net, basket and other essential paraphernalia was designed to leave little doubt in the eyes of the casual observer as to the purpose of my visit to these parts.

'The river's down that way. You be going away from it.'

I thanked the whiskery old gentleman for his advice. I could have explained to him that, like any seasoned huntsman, I was merely reconnoitring the lie of the land upon which my great hunt would be played out. I could have explained to him that my prey was not a fish. I could have explained to him that my prey was man—more deadly than the trout. But as he struck me as more than usually dense—in a noble, rustic sort of way—I felt that the process would intrude too much upon my time. Besides, I had no wish to reveal to anyone my true intent. Raising my hat to him (and pricking my finger on one of the many fine flies that adorned it), I set my face towards the river and towards the honest yeomen of England that do their business in the great waters of the Thames.

I needn't have bothered.

'How's business?' I asked cheerily of the first Thames-man I met, evidently the proprietor of the anglers' shop he sat in front of.

'I wouldn't know about yours. And I like to mind me own,' he said.

I decided to ignore this man's manners for the sake of the greater quest.

'Tell me, my good man,' I said. 'Have you seen any strangers round here recently? Anyone suspicious, furtive, looking like he's up to no good? Anyone at all like that?'

'Oh, yes, I have that. Don't you worry.'

'Really? When did you see him? Last Tuesday by any chance?'

'No. More recent than that.'

Could it be possible? Had my quarry doubled back on himself to throw off his pursuers, and was he far closer than I had imagined? Was he perhaps now the hunter, and I the hunted?

'When, man? When was this?' I asked urgently.

'Oh, this morning.'

This very morning!

'And where did you spot him?'

'Oh, I'd say… pretty much where you're standing

now. Arr, pretty much exact.' He gave himself a self-satisfied chuckle and I perceived the nature of this worthless fellow's jest.

'And I suppose he was wearing something like my clothes?' I asked coldly.

'Oh, bless me, sir. Now you come to mention it I'd say he wore clothes exact like those. Exact. Ha, ha, ha!'

He threw his head back in uncontrollable mirth, toppled backwards off his stool, and hit the ground hard. He was still laughing. This story, however, had a sad ending. I learned later that he was quite unharmed by his fall.

The sheer rudeness of the countryman towards his city-born betters can be quite breathtaking. I wonder if there is not something in the very air of the country that turns ordinary men into beasts, and yeomen into churls. Did our forefathers not show great wisdom in turning words for country-dwellers, villain and heathen, for example, into labels of opprobrium? Give me civilization over the countryside any day of the week.

The other inhabitants of Pangbourne, it must frankly be admitted, were little more helpful than the angling shop proprietor. Some could not remember further back than the day before. Others gave wonderfully detailed descriptions of visitors, who upon further inquiry turned out to have visited many years ago. It was only when I called at the charming village post office that I met with more acute powers of observation, and the very information I sought, in the responses of the officer of the post himself.

'Last Tuesday, did you say, sir? Now I think of it there was a strange man come in that day. An old soldier, he was. Very shabbily dressed. Had a patch over his left eye. Had a peg-leg—his right, I think—and walked with a big stick, more of a staff, if you know what I mean. He brought a stamp and left a letter for delivery. Can't remember the address.'

'Well, thank you. That sounds just like my long-lost uncle Toby,' I said, and to express my gratitude bought a set of picture postcards of Pangbourne and environs. 'I shall be on my way.'

'Just a minute, sir. I've remembered something else about your uncle. He had a small animal in a cage. A ferret I think it was. No—I tell a lie: it was a mongoose, 'cause I remember asking the old gent what it was. A mongoose, definitely.'

'A mongoose? That's bizarre—I mean to say, my uncle Toby is nothing if not eccentric. Thank you, my man.'

'My pleasure, sir. Oh, there was just one other thing.'

'Yes?' I asked, desperate to know every last detail. 'What exactly *is* a mongoose, sir?'

*　　*　　*

My quarry was now within my grasp, and it was with a light heart that I took dinner at a charming inn before turning back to Pangbourne station and my afternoon rendezvous with Harris. Mrs Hudson's plan was working perfectly—so far.

Chapter Nine

THE SECOND REPORT OF DR JOHN H.
WATSON, SIX DAYS EARLIER

The Abbey Hotel,
Abingdon,
Friday 6 June

M Y dear Holmes,
    The good news is that I am still in contact
with our friend 'Jan'. At Oxford he hired a boat as
planned. But he is no river-man, and even though
I took my scull out a good twenty minutes after his
departure, he was still to be found in midstream
rowing in circles. I think he must never have rowed
before, and that the decision, whether his own or
that of a superior, to adopt this mode of transport
is a poor one: he is succeeding only in drawing
attention to himself. Moreover, it is difficult as well
as tiresome to pursue a man on the river whose
main direction of travel is circular: he is as likely
to end up following you as you him. And finally, it
should be noted for any further adventures of this

sort that of all craft the standard rowing boat is the least well-adapted for covert pursuit. One cannot see one's prey—except by continually looking over one's shoulder in a manner almost guaranteed to reveal both one's identity and purpose—while all the time you are clearly in his sight.

I therefore rowed considerably ahead of my prey, and 'followed' him from in front. This is a far more satisfactory arrangement. Or it would have been, except for the fact that when over-hauling him, in an awkward pose calculated to conceal my face from view, I pulled a muscle in my shoulder. As ill-luck would have it, it is the same shoulder which had been struck by a Jezail bullet in Afghanistan. I am now in some pain, which I suspect is exacerbated by the effect of the damp atmosphere, and have therefore engaged an eskimo canoe for tomorrow's work, and surrendered the single-scull to the local boat hire firm (luckily they are the same company as the Oxford one). It is a lighter, faster craft in which the rower—or rather paddler—faces forwards, and it will allow me to continue my quest with greater ease and less physical strain.

Chapter Ten

An incredible coincidence—The improbability of mothers-in-law—A peculiarity of the English—Women not the gentler sex, proven by observation—The importance of reading public notices—An expensive lesson

Thursday 13 June

I T was mid-afternoon in Maidenhead, and Harris and I were sitting in a picturesque pub garden, at a table placed up against the back wall of the pub. The pub garden was doing a brisk trade that afternoon, with quite a few cooing couples in attendance. I dare say they had tried to get in at more fashionable places, but on account of the great over-supply of cooing couples in Maidenhead at that time of year, had been forced to rough it in this dusty but charming locale. Having taken the essential precaution of arming ourselves with a glass of Bass each, Harris and I were exchanging notes on our morning's investigations along the Thames. Harris had just said something that astounded me.

'But this is incredible, Harris! They cannot be the same man, and yet it is impossible that there could be three such as they on the river!'

'I had it from two witnesses, J. One in the pub, the other in Goring post office. And I wrote down what they said as soon as I could in each case. Here it is in black and white: the one seen in the pub was described as 'Battered old soldier. Patch on left eye. Twisted lip. Accompanied by distinctive foreign-looking pygmy he called "my Andaman friend".' The one seen in the post office was 'Old soldier with patch on right eye, false left leg, crutch under left arm, with trained otter who followed him everywhere, at times on a lead, at others walking to heel like a dog.'

'Could he be the same man, altering his appearance each time to throw off a pursuer?' I asked. It was, I confess, an odd scenario I was essaying. But I have long maintained that, until something is proved to be absolutely impossible, it must always be held to be possible, no matter how improbable it may be—as the man said when he met his prospective mother-in-law for the first time.

'It's not much of a change of disguise, is it, J.? For the Thames, I mean,' replied Harris. 'Besides, you are supposing that he has an unending supply of short foreign friends and exotic pets.'

'Perhaps the pygmy ordinarily looks after the animals,' I suggested, without much conviction.

'Then we are looking for a pet-shop or menagerie somewhere in the Thames Valley run by an expatriate Andaman Islander. That shouldn't be too hard to track down.'

'No, it shouldn't…' I said absent-mindedly, for at that moment my eye was drawn to a figure who had just entered the pub garden. He was an old soldier, evidently down on his luck. He wore dirty bandages around his head, held in place by an antique kilmarnock with renewed chinstrap, and a straggly beard more white than grey. He walked with a crutch under his left arm, and carried a cage with a canary in it, singing sweetly. (The canary was singing sweetly, not the ex-serviceman.) He was begging baksheesh from table to table, and soon he would be level with our own.

The Lord had delivered mine enemy into my hands good and proper, and I was determined to settle this once and for all, whatever the cost. He drew close, and I waited until his attention was distracted by a pretty girl reaching into her purse for him. If this fellow were anything like the London branch of his firm who had visited my rooms the previous day, he would be devious and desperate, with a thousand tricks up his tattered and torn sleeve. I needed every advantage I could charm to my side, of which surprise is always chiefest. I therefore leapt at him with all my strength, and we both went crashing to the ground before the pretty girl's table.

'What are you doing? Let me go! Get off me!' shouted the imposter.

'I shall, my friend, I shall. Just as soon as you tell me what your name is, what foreign government you are working for, and why you have been sending threatening messages to Briony Lodge!'

The imposter cleverly avoided my charges.

'He's a madman. Someone help me!' he shouted to those at the tables around us.

It is a peculiarity of the English that though, when taken singly, they can normally be relied to act with a degree of commonsense that is the envy of the world, when in a crowd all prudence leaves them. It is also a still-common misconception to hail the female of the human species as the gentler sex. In fact, it is they who are mediately responsible for the majority of broken noses, black eyes, cut lips, and grazed knuckles one sees on men around town of a Monday morning. And so it was that I, who should have been carried round Maidenhead as the toast of the town, found myself being handled roughly by two oafs wearing striped blazers, while their pretty companions fussed around the bearded tramp.

'Oh, you poor old gentleman!' said one young charmer. 'Here, have my champagne. It always makes me feel so much better.'

'Oh, look, Charles!' said the other dear charmer. 'That hooligan has made this gentleman drop his birdcage. And look—his poor little bird—a feather has come loose! A feather, Charles! That man is a brute!'

Charles was squaring up to punch me on the nose. Harris was not by my side—in fact, from the corner of my eye I could see that he had suddenly become fascinated by an old poster pasted on the wall above our table. I was alone. I had to act fast and decisively.

'Ha, you poor dupes!' I shouted, hoping to gain the attention of the whole garden. 'You think this man is a harmless old soldier. A hero, perhaps, who fought for Queen and country. I tell you he is nothing of the sort. Quite the opposite: he is a German—yes, and he has been terrorizing a young English schoolmistress by the name of Briony Lodge. And if you do not believe me, then believe the evidence of your own eyes!' At this, I lunged forward and grabbed the man's straggly white beard.

The beard did not budge.

I pulled and pulled in vain, the only result being that the imposter cried all the louder.

'You are a bounder, sir,' fumed Charles. 'You come here and knock that innocent man off his feet, cause his canary to lose a feather,'—here he glanced back to make sure that his belle was still admiring him—'and then try to pull off his beard. It will be a pleasure to strike you, sir. In fact, I hate your sort, the type of city swell who fills up the best hotels so no-one else can book a room. Then you come here and think you can behave as you like. Well you can't, and my strong right arm will prove my point. Why, I even bet you're here with some floozy, aren't you? Does your wife know that you two are here together? Because I've a mind to tell her when I get back to town. And to tell her I gave you a good thrashing.'

Some people can be so censorious, so judgmental, about their fellow-man, so eager to cast the first stone, that it can be quite appalling to hear it.

At this point my hirsute victim addressed his new champion.

'God bless you, sir. If this whippersnapper had tried it on with me twenty year ago, he'd have known about it all right. But in my state—well, I thank you for coming to my rescue. As for being a German spy, I've never even left Berkshire, except in the service of my Queen, God bless her. I don't even speak Germanish. I'm here for the annual rally. Look!'

He was pointing to the large, gaudy poster in red and blue ink on white background that Harris was still steadfastly perusing.

NATIONAL ANNUAL CONVENTION OF
INJURED EX-SERVICEMEN
Brave sailors and soldiers of Britain!
Answer the call once more!
Come to Maidenhead on Friday 14 June!
Wear your wounds and medals with pride!
ENGLAND EXPECTS YOU THIS DAY!

'He's right, you know, J.,' announced Harris unnecessarily. 'The poster says that nurses, companions, and companion animals are particularly welcome.'

The light had dawned, and I went over to the old hero.

'I'm… I'm very sorry, sir,' I said. 'I mistook you for another man who looks very like you. I hope that no harm has been done.' I offered my hand to help lift the dignified old man to his feet.

'No harm? No harm!' spluttered Charles, before the man had had chance to reply. 'You half kill him then say "No harm done"? You owe him more than an apology, you… you city poltroon! Give him some of your money for his trouble. Unless you want Edgar and me to teach you a lesson you won't forget.'

I had no choice but to fish out my pocket-book.

'More than that,' Edgar broke in. 'What about his hurt feelings?'

Edgar must be a lawyer, I decided, as I handed over another note.

'And what about his poor canary?' said Charles's young lady. 'It deserves the very finest medical attention, and I don't suppose that comes cheap, does it, Charles?' She looked at Charles coquettishly.

Charles must be a medic, I decided, as I handed over two more notes.

All in all, it was the most expensive visit I ever made to a public house. But then, I *was* with Harris.

Chapter Eleven

The Dog and Duck,
Goring,
Sunday 8th June

M Y dear Holmes,
Today's proceedings have been as full of
incident as we could have wished or feared. I only
hope that my pen can do justice to the high drama
of the day.

This morning at Wallingford I waited for Jan
to emerge from his hotel (The Angel) and walk the
short distance to the landing stage where his boat
was moored. When eight o'clock (the time of his
start from Abingdon the previous day) had come
and gone, I began to worry. It was of course perfectly natural for an inexperienced rower to rest as
long as he could after such unaccustomed exertion.
For that matter, my own shoulder was glad of the
enforced idleness. On the other hand, it is never

good news for the predator when his prey changes his behaviour. Had he humbugged me? A hasty check revealed that Jan's boat was still at its mooring. But what if Jan himself had risen early and already left Wallingford by some other means?

This thought so nagged at me that at last I resolved to enter his hotel even at the risk of my being seen by him yet again. He must have seen me already in the Botanic Gardens, where I would have been distinguished by my dress, age, and moustaches from the languid, clean-shaven, black-cloaked Adonises of Magdalen who were the only other visitors at that hour. He was certain to have seen me on the river, unless he really were more focussed on rowing than his lack of linear progress suggested. Entering the lobby with heart in mouth, I approached the small reception desk and, under cover of making some commonplace inquiry, observed that none of the guest room keys was hanging on its peg. An equally discreet reconnaissance of the grounds proved that there was no way out that did not lead directly into the road I was watching.

There was nothing for it but to continue my siege of Jan's hotel, from cover and a safe distance, until his departure. There was a good deal of traffic in and out of the hotel, but none involved Jan. I began to wonder whether he had not flitted from the hotel without settling his bill or returning his key. The man was after all an anarchist, a conspirator, a blackmailer and a potential assassin, who would surely not blanch at the thought of decamping without payment. But after forty minutes I was rewarded by the sight of Jan leaving. He was not alone, and he did not direct his steps to the river as I had expected. Instead, he made his way towards me, in the company of two men who had called at the hotel about ten minutes before. The new men were certainly striking in appearance—both were tall and powerfully built, and one had hair the colour of snow above a bronzed, out-doors face. He carried a suitcase and a smaller attaché case, his friend a large gladstone and what looked like a bundle of fishing rods and a net wrapped in a waterproof. Jan had his usual small bundle with him, and an envelope, which he posted in the wall-box outside the hotel as they passed.

They crossed the road and made towards me with a purposeful step. I had taken cover in a thicket on rising ground above the point at which a narrow path forks off the main lane from the river and strikes into dense woodland. For a long moment, I thought that they had spotted me and were anxious to hold an old-fashioned conversation. I thought to run, but I did not rate my chances very highly with the two hefty newcomers if they caught me in the open, and I decided that I was safer in my den. But it became evident that they were simply seeking the solitude of the wood, for they turned off the lane and walked a little along the path. Here they were invisible from the lane but not from me. They began to speak in hushed, hurried tones in a guttural language I supposed to be Czech or German. At length, the white-haired man motioned to his companion who produced a neatly-tied brown paper parcel and handed it to Jan. Leaving the well-wrapped fishing gear and the large gladstone, the companion then went towards the road, took up a central position on the path, and adopted such a menacing stance as would have deterred the most seasoned habitué of woodland walks from venturing upon that track. Meanwhile, the white-haired man moved up the path in the opposite direction, presumably to perform a similar obstructive function.

Jan had now unwrapped the parcel. As I had predicted, it contained a change of clothes. What I could not have predicted—although I suspect that the matter would have seemed quite straightforward to you, Holmes—was that the clothes would be older and dirtier than those he was wearing! He removed his foreign-looking but otherwise perfectly decent set and changed to a set that no self-respecting tramp would have looked at twice—torn trousers, filthy shirt, and tattered military jacket. I was astonished by this transformation, but more was to come. White-hair returned and opened the neat attaché case. Jan stood patiently as White-hair transfigured him before my eyes. False sideburns and eyebrows were applied by spirit gum; one side of his upper-lip was lifted and affixed by a self-adhesive plaster, giving Jan a permanent sneer; and finally *maquillage* was applied and thirty careworn years of hardship were instantly etched upon Jan's face, together with a couple of weeping pustules of more than usually horrid appearance, difficult to behold even for a medical man like myself. Various other defects were added to neck, arms, and legs, and Jan was transformed into the sort of man that no-one would pay, or want to pay, close attention to—one of the offscourings of humanity who inspires pity in all hearts, but who repels rather than attracts. In short, a perfect disguise for one who wishes to pass unnoticed through life.

I wondered afterwards why this intricate metamorphosis had not been undertaken in the privacy and convenience of Jan's hotel room rather than the open air, where there was at least some chance of being discovered in the act. But then I reflected that it would have been difficult indeed for the transformed Jan to have exited through the lobby of such a respectable establishment, and still less have settled his account, without attracting a good deal of attention. The departure of such a foul-looking apparition through the kitchen area at the back would have attracted even more attention, and a black eye or two into the bargain. And so this mysterious party—now become considerably more mysterious—had no choice but to use the small clearing below me as an impromptu dressing-room.

One might have thought that the morning had seen enough strange goings-on already. But there was more to come that, if anything, was stranger still. First, White-hair's companion gave Jan what I had taken to be a bundle of fishing rods and a net. In fact, what emerged from the wrappings was nothing more—or less—than a T-shaped crutch, with a very substantial shaft and a cross bar well padded and tightly strapped. Jan tried it out and was soon moving as fluently as any man with one sound leg might. But what happened next topped all the events of the morning. Out of his capacious gladstone, the companion withdrew a cage, within which was a docile, still sleeping, animal. Once it was out of the cage, safely on a lead, it woke and started sniffing out the riverside smells. I recognized it immediately as an otter. It was obvious that this was also supposed to be part of Jan's new disguise. It struck me as a touch too far. Without the otter, Jan could have passed anywhere as a more than usually repellent beggar, and therefore anonymous. With the otter, he became 'the beggar with an otter', a man whom people could identify and talk about. Our Bohemian friends were clever, of that there is no doubt. But it occurred to me at that moment that they had overplayed their hand.

What happened next? It is easily told. The three friends each lit and smoked cigarettes, in celebration of a job well done, then parted with handshakes and back-slapping all round. Almost as an afterthought, White-hair opened his suitcase and handed Jan what looked like a bar of fancy eating chocolate with a red wrapper. Jan was presumably delighted to receive this gift, but his expression of gratitude succeeded only in making a horribly distorted face more horribly distorted. White-hair and his companion made for the railway station, while Jan fed the otter a meal of what looked like white fish before hobbling off with his new friend in the direction of the Reading road. At length, when all was clear, I emerged from the hide which had served me so well. I descended to the clearing, and sought out the cigarette ends left by the anarchists, in case this information might be of assistance in tracking them in future. You would,

I hope, have been proud of me for thinking of this. I became excited when I spotted what I took to be the remains of a distinctive long, thin black Russian cigarette. Unfortunately, closer inspection revealed it to be something the otter had necessarily left behind after his hours spent in a gladstone bag.

My next move was obvious. I had overheard the conspirators refer more than once to Goring. It is such a naturally German-sounding word that at first it did not occur to me that they meant the pleasant riverside village which looks across the Thames to its twin, Streatly. It was evident that that was Jan's next destination. He would be on foot, or rather hobbling on a crutch, and so I would easily be able to reach Goring by canoe, secure my lodgings for the night, take lunch, and position myself to observe Jan's arrival.

That is what I did, and all went according to plan, but for one extraordinary occurrence. I was sitting down to lunch in my new billet, The Dog and Duck, when a distinguished-looking man in a window-table beckoned me across. It was a half-minute before I recognized my superior officer in the Royal Berkshire Regiment, Major (now Lieutenant-Colonel) Henry Haversham. (You will remember that I joined the Fifth Northumberland Fusiliers, but found myself attached to the Berkshires at the time of the Maiwand campaign). We got talking about old times, as old soldiers inevitably do. He, it transpired, had carved out a career for himself in the police after leaving the army, and was now indeed the Chief Constable of the county. He still lived in his splendid family seat, two miles or so from Goring. But tragedy had struck home within the last twelvemonth, taking from him his dear wife and daughter. The great house had become distasteful to him, but he could no more think of selling up than of cutting off his right arm. And so on Sundays, when the solitude of the place, and memories of happier times, hung heavy upon him and he had not the distractions of work to help, he had taken to having lunch at this hotel in Goring.

It was indeed a sad tale to hear, for Henry was a good officer and an even better man, and I could not help but offer a silent prayer of thanksgiving for the many blessings of my own life.

Then the conversation turned to me, and I explained as best I could (and as discreetly, given our public venue) the nature of my mission. Spoken out loud, the fact that I was canoeing down the Thames in pursuit of a man dressed as a lame beggar with an otter, sounded so fantastical that for a moment I feared that Henry might think me to have gone off my head. Instead, a look of extreme concentration descended upon his features. He had seen a communiqué from the Oxfordshire force on Friday about this very matter. He had given it no more thought at the time, being as it was a routine notification to a neighbouring force of a matter of common interest. But now he knew that his old battalion medic was involved, he promised to mobilize every last man in the Berkshire Constabulary, if need be, to assist.

I was delighted to hear this. The arrival of Whitehair and his equally hefty accomplice upon the scene had weighted the die firmly against me. Not only was I heavily out-gunned if it came to violence, but my enemies now had the option of laying two false trails. I was no longer sure that Jan, in his elaborate disguise, was not himself now a decoy, though my instincts told me that I was still, for the time being, on the right track. Henry mentioned a new unit he had set up which seemed perfect for this situation. It was a squad of specially-trained plain-clothes constables under a sergeant, all mounted on fast bicycles—the 'flying squad', he called it—and which could outrun any moving object except a train. He promised to assign them to the case immediately he returned home, using the special electrical telephone which had been installed in his house and which connected directly to the principal divisional headquarters.

As Henry spoke, the old spark I remembered as his most distinctive characteristic returned to his eyes. He was a man who flourished on work, without which he was bound to dwell too much upon his misfortunes. So I was glad to have been the bringer of this challenge. But as we were leaving, he said a remarkable thing to me. Shaking my hand, he asked after my old injury, then suggested light-heartedly that if I got bored I could always go to Maidenhead on Friday and join the other wounded old soldiers.

Wounded old soldiers! I instantly grasped the full import of this news. Jan's new disguise was not that of any old tramp but specifically that of an old soldier down on his luck. Far from being overly-theatrical, as I had thought, such a disguise would be of the greatest utility, for at that moment a brigade of wounded ex-servicemen was converging upon Maidenhead. There Jan could be sure of throwing off any pursuers in the general melee. My admiration of the cleverness of our enemy rose to new heights.

Luckily, I was able to secure at the Dog and Duck a room that overlooked the Oxford Road, and Jan hove into view just ten minutes after the time I had estimated for his arrival. I readied myself to follow him in order to ascertain his overnight billet, wondering if he would dare enter a regular hotel wearing such garb and with an animal, when I was stopped in my tracks. Jan was making straight for the Dog and Duck! I tiptoed out onto the landing which overlooked the hallway below in order to overhear the conversation, and half expected to hear the porter summoned to throw poor Jan and his otter out on their ears. But I had underestimated the patriotism of the Goring hotelier. Arrangements were made to house the otter in the proprietor's daughter's rabbit cage (no mention of what alternative arrangements the rabbit would have to make), and the sham old soldier himself was given a room on the ground floor. I withdrew silently, and decided to make a start of writing up the extraordinary events of this day.

Chapter Twelve

A discussion between friends—Harris's strange metamorphosis—A riverside disquisition upon continental chocolate—The tale of a false affliction and a true otter

---

'IT was your bally fault, Harris. What are friends for if not to back you up?'

'No, J. It was *your* bally fault. You should never have attacked that old man. If you'd read that poster like me, instead of slurping your ale like a pig in a trough…'

'Slurping? Slurping! I'll have you know that I hardly moistened my lips on that pint—and it cost me twenty quid! Moreover, I'll have you know that…'

'Oh, look, J., there's an injured old soldier ahead of us. What do you reckon—bring him down with a rugby tackle or simply cosh him over the back of his head? I'm sure you brought a life-preserver with you—you seem to have brought most of Baker Street along for this overnight trip. If you can't find the life-preserver, I'm sure we could do just as good a job with the umbrella stand or the kitchen-sink. I've seen them both in your luggage somewhere.'

Had anyone overheard our amiable conversation as we took an early evening walk along the river at Maidenhead, they might conceivably have mistaken it for something more heated. In fact, it was the sort of conversation only *true* friends can have. I feel rather sorry for those who cannot have them.

Some yards ahead of us, as Harris had correctly observed, strolled another evening promenader, an old soldier with a crutch and an otter on a lead. He was possibly the same man that Harris had heard about in the post office at Goring. But, on the matter of injured ex-servicemen, I was understandably reluctant to leap to any conclusions. My recollection of the proceedings in the pub garden that afternoon were too fresh and too painful. Especially as concerns the twenty pounds. Much further behind us was a gaggle of bicyclists whose object appeared to be to ride as slowly as possible without actually falling over or wobbling off into the river. I was about to suggest to Harris that we tarry to watch them, just to cheer ourselves up by attending to other people's misfortunes, when he stopped in his tracks and stared dead ahead.

In order to comprehend the remarkable, and indeed tragic, sequence of events that was about to unfold, the reader needs to grasp the import of one fact above all: Harris's allergy to litter. Seeing litter about the street causes Harris to metamorphose from a mostly likeable fellow into a very fiend from Hell. But seeing someone purposely drop litter—especially if they do it openly and nonchalantly rather than surreptitiously and guiltily like any civilized man—conjures up all his most sadistic and murderous tendencies. Torquemada suffered in much the same way, I understand, except that in his case it was heresy that brought the old problem on. Still, it takes all sorts to make a world, as my old aunt used to say, and who are we to judge?

'Did you see what that otter-fellow just did, J.?' Harris hissed. 'He threw that wrapper onto the riverbank. He must be some kind of animal!'

'Perhaps it was the otter that did it. *He* really is an animal,' I replied, trying vainly to suppress the eruption to come. But it was no more use than expecting a pretty girl not to sneeze just because you have offered her your best handkerchief.

As we drew level with the discarded red wrapper, Harris stopped to pick it up. I knew from experience what he intended to do, but this time there was a twist. He read the wrapper.

"'Die Hamburgerischeschokoladevereinsgesell-
schaft',' he announced. '"Schokolade." So British
chocolate is not good enough for our ottery friend.
So we are above British chocolate, are we? Is that
not perhaps because we are not British? Tell me, J.,
what sort of a man deliberately eats Hun chocolate?
Belgian chocolate, French chocolate, Swiss chocolate: those are international chocolates, accepted
the world over. Anyone may eat of such chocolate
regardless of nationality, without attracting undue
attention. But only a German could possibly enjoy
German chocolate. There is your villain, J.; there the
tormentor-in-chief of the fair Briony. Your duty is
clear. Do it. If not, I shall.'

My pacific friend, who had carelessly read a
poster while my life and limb were being threatened by louts, had disappeared. In his place was a
fire-born dragon from the very bowels of Hades. I
do wish people would consider the consequences
before they discard their rubbish in a public place.

'Steady on, old chap. You can't possibly know
that. Just because of a chocolate wrapper.'

Harris had quickened his pace and I had hurried
after, and we were now just a few steps behind our
man. The otter was the first to notice our approach,
and cast a worried backward glance at us, before
scurrying for safety through his master's legs. The

man himself, lost in his own thoughts, heard not
our approach. In view of what was to happen, I take
some comfort in the knowledge that he had, in his
no doubt troubled life, found some serenity at last
in this quiet summer evening's promenade along the
river. For all I know, he had made his peace with
his Maker, and his conscience was clear and his soul
ready for whatever fate had in store for him. We can
hope no more than the same for ourselves, when
our time comes.

'Very well, then, J.,' said Harris. 'You may shirk
your patriotic duty, but let not the same be said of
me. Guten Abend, mein Herr!' he called out. The
man in front, still many miles away in blissful day-
dreams, half-turned, smiled, and returned the 'guten
Abend'. Then he froze as he realized his mistake.

'Kennen Sie vielleicht Briony Lodge, mein Herr?'

At these words of Harris's, our adversary turned
fully upon us, took his heavy crutch and flung it
at our legs. We got considerably tangled up in it,
and he saw his opportunity to escape us on his two
perfectly good feet. He might have got away, too,
but for a peculiarity of that stretch of the river. We
were level with the lip of the first in a series of weirs,
which shelved gently enough to begin with but soon
degenerated into falls of a most un-Berkshire-like
violence. Out of the corner of his eye, the otter

must have seen an enormous trout in the shallow water of the lip—the sort you never see when you go looking for them, but which swim to the bank in great fishy flocks when you have no rod in your hand, and ask you for biscuits. At this, the otter's training deserted him (assuming that he had ever been certificated for riverside promenading in the first place, which in retrospect I rather doubt). He straightaway dived into the river after his supper. Unfortunately, the effect of his earlier scurryings back and forth had been to wrap the lead around his master's legs. Where the otter went, the man was obliged to follow. And so the two of them leapt into the river, the second far less gracefully than the first.

I heard later that the otter, whom I have every reason to believe was a patriotic but deeply misled fellow, was found unharmed a mile downstream. He was sitting on a rock by the riverbank, minus lead but still wearing his collar, preening himself and looking considerably glossier and fatter. Of the trout, only a few of the larger bones remained, scattered about the rock. The German had been concussed by his fall and had drowned. He was found floating peacefully on his back, all the troubles and betrayals and villainies of his life now quite soothed away by the kindly, cold hand of Death.

Chapter Thirteen

Thursday 13 June

T HIS day has been a bitter-sweet one for me.
Sweet, because my mission is at an end and I
will soon be reunited with my beloved Mary. Bitter,
because the man I have been following since Oxford
is no more.

In just the same way that one can learn much
about the character of a fellow chess-player from a
couple of games, without ever exchanging a word, I
feel that I came to know Jan by observing him and
attempting to anticipate his next move. Although
he was a conspirator and, I do not doubt, a black-
guard, I came—I admit it—to like the fellow! His
determination and devotion, however misguided
his cause, endeared him to me. But now his body
lies on a mortuary slab in Maidenhead, and my
signature on the certificate gives his cause of death
as 'Otter'. The creature whose entrance upon the

scene was, in my view, a step too far down the road of legitimate disguise in the direction of amateur theatrics, caused Jan to lose his own step, fall into the river, and drown.

Holmes, for all his marvellous gifts, cannot see his opponents, or even those he agrees to help, as real people in this way. To him, they are merely values and factors in a mathematical equation that needs solving. If, like Jan, they are subtracted or cancelled out, that just simplifies the equation. He knows *of* love and jealousy and hatred and greed, and can manipulate them to his advantage: indeed, how many are the maidservants of great houses that he has made love to for the information they could provide him, and who still daily expect him to return to claim them? But he himself has never felt the pang of such passions, and so considers himself above the generality which does. To be sure, he knows boredom, and adopts measures against it which I find reprehensible; but of other human emotions he is as *personally* ignorant as he is of the rotation of the earth about the sun. I could almost wish that one day he might suffer a reverse, a failure, and learn more of normal human feelings in that one instant than through all the penny-dreadfuls and lurid police reports he has ever read. I would not wish him to fail on any great matter of state, of course, or in the pursuit of any murderer or other vicious felon, but in some token but memorable way. And if it could be at the hands of someone he ordinarily despises—a woman, perhaps—so much the better. Perhaps Miss Irene Adler herself might prove his equal. But I daydream, and of course I wish Holmes no harm or lack of success. I just wish he could be more human.

But let me bring some order to my account, if I cannot yet bring it to my conflicting emotions, by starting at the beginning. That Jan's destination was to be Maidenhead, there was no disputing. His latest disguise clearly marked him out as one intending to lose himself in the crowd of invalids converging on the annual national convention of war-wounded. Once there, he no doubt intended to adopt a third disguise and slip away discreetly, continuing his mission against the King of Bohemia.

My old friend Henry Haversham, now Chief Constable of Berkshire, had promised me the services of his plain-clothed bicycle-mounted division based at Reading. They were able not only to monitor Jan's progress as he neared Maidenhead, but to report back at regular intervals by relay, and then by means of telephonic communication, so that I was kept constantly informed in a most impressive manner. When Jan was reported to be in Maidenhead, I was invited to join the ranks of Henry's 'flying squad', which I was happy to do.

The officer in charge of the mounted division, Sergeant Gruffudd, was all for arresting our quarry there and then. He reasoned that once Jan melted into the crowds of invalid ex-servicemen, he would be very difficult to spot again. I had to accept the wisdom of his view, but Holmes's own strict instructions had been to follow and observe, not to interfere. That approach had, it was true, brought to light the existence of the two accomplices, and it might yield more fruit yet. Yet the sergeant's cautious approach had obvious merit, and whatever the nature of Jan's intentions towards Miss Adler and the King of Bohemia, he was now a good deal nearer his destination, and there was no guarantee that we could pick up his scent again in time. But on what grounds could he be detained? I was not sure that Jan had committed any crime so far. Sergeant Gruffudd assured me that he could think of a dozen charges, ranging from intention to defraud to several offences relating to the keeping of wild animals. The Reading police are certainly thorough.

Even as we were debating such matters, events were already moving rapidly to their tragic conclusion. We saw up ahead that Jan had stopped to speak to two young gentlemen we had seen strolling behind him. Then he seemed to take fright, and threw his walking-crutch at them, scattering them like nine-pins. As one man, we began to pedal furiously, but before we had reached the scene Jan—still imbalanced by the throwing of the crutch and now pulled off his feet by the escaping otter, fell into the river.

The body was carried down river fast, and there was no question of leaping in after him. Instead, I joined a section of the cyclists who raced after the body. But I could see Jan's body drifting unprotesting downstream, and already I knew in my heart that my mission was over. The majority of the squad—whose ranks were now swelled by Thames Conservancy and other officials, to insure that jurisdictional boundaries were not crossed—stopped to detain and question the young men: they were not responsible for what had happened, but they had clearly said something to Jan which caused him to react violently.

His body came to rest against an old tree trunk jammed against the further bank. Strange to relate, when we found him the otter, who was most to blame for the incident, but who was hardly criminally culpable, was sitting on the opposite bank alongside its former master. Whether he meant to mourn his master's corpse or to eat it I could not tell. He is now free to roam the Thames, and will no doubt make himself as unpopular amongst anglers as he already is amongst the trout.

So that is the end of the story, but for a singular postscript. I had noticed and recognized the two young gentlemen who had incurred Jan's wrath as none other than Holmes's upstairs neighbours from Baker Street! Once the medical formalities had been completed and Jan's body carried off to the mortuary, I returned to Sergeant Gruffudd and informed him of this. I suggested that he look for a third man, George Wingrave, who was Harris's and Jerome's constant companion. The local hotels were all checked, without success, but Sergeant Gruffudd had the excellent idea of checking at the post office for any *poste restante* mail. He asked me to come with him, and I soon discovered his reason for asking. It is a relatively minor offence for a member of the public to open a letter intended for someone else. But if it became known that a policeman had done the same, even in the process of investigating a crime, it would be likely to bring about the complete collapse of public faith in the police throughout the Kingdom. I was at first reluctant to participate in this subterfuge, but was relieved to see that the contents of the letter completely exonerated the three of any complicity in the plot. They had somehow become involved in it, but fortunately were far too ignorant to understand it.

I was treated to an example of this ignorance when I went to free Harris and Jerome from Maidenhead gaol. I gave a description of their identities, address (Jerome's, at least), and occupations, and they stood there quite astonished, as if I were some clairvoyant who had supernatural access to such secrets. It clearly did not occur to them that Mrs Hudson chats incessantly about the other tenants of 221 Baker Street, at least when under medical examination. As the pair stood there open-mouthed in amazement, I could not help but recall Holmes's favourite line from Tacitus—*omne ignotum pro magnifico*. Well, it might be useful to keep those boisterous neighbours in awe of my magical reputation for a little longer, so I shall say nothing to spoil the delicate bloom of their ignorance.

Chapter Fourteen

The correct treatment of policemen—The
extraordinary power of Briony Lodge's name

No sooner had the unfortunate foreigner struck the lip of the weir than Harris and I were surrounded by the bicyclists, who had suddenly shown a turn of speed with which I should never have credited them. A group dashed off downstream after the German (as we still supposed him to be), who was being dragged by the current; the rest hemmed us in. The leader of the group introduced himself.

'Good evening, gentlemen. My name is Sergeant David Gruffudd of the Reading City Police Mounted Division (River Company), and these are my men. Also present are Sergeant Poole of the Maidenhead Police and Mr Antrobus of the Thames Conservancy Board. We have detained you in order to ask you a few questions about your activities on the river bank, and in particular your connection with the man who has just taken a swim.'

'Good evening, Sergeant,' I replied, reasoning that it was always as well to remain polite with policemen until it became absolutely imperative to show firmness. They are rather like dogs in that respect, especially when in a pack.

'Now I noticed that you addressed the gentleman. You said something to him that made him throw his crutch at you and then throw himself in the river, to what I suspect was his certain death.'

At the mention of death, the Thames Conservancy man looked downstream and nodded gravely.

'Do you mind telling me what it was you said?'

'Not at all, Sergeant,' said Harris, who had recovered a more equable temperament. 'I said, "Guten Abend, mein Herr". It means "Good evening, sir". In German.'

'Thank you, sir. As it happens, and despite what the Maidenhead boys say, the Reading police are not completely ignorant. We have a very competent foreign language unit back at division, and they do provide us with sufficient knowledge to keep up with the lingo of our summer visitors. What made you think he was German, sir?'

'Because of this,' said Harris, handing over the chocolate wrapper, which he had smoothed out and folded neatly into a pocket of his blazer.

'I see, sir. And did you say anything else to him before he flung himself into the river?'

'Yes, I said "Kennen Sie vielleicht…". I asked him if by chance he knew Briony Lodge.'

'Indeed, sir? This is most gratifying to hear. Most gratifying indeed.'

'Why so, Sergeant?'

'Because it means I get to say this: "I arrest you both in the name of the Queen". That is English, sir, for "You're nicked".'

Chapter Fifteen

Spacious, unfurnished Georgian room to let, central Maidenhead area—The predictable dialogue of young swains in love—The lethality of the straw boater—The Scylla of melodrama and the Charybdis of sentiment both successfully avoided—The salutary effects of reading other people's private correspondence

HARRIS and I did not return to our hastily-arranged but comfortable hotel in Maidenhead that evening. Instead, we found ourselves persuaded to try out the 'holding cell' at Maidenhead Police Station. Its name admirably indicates to prospective guests exactly what to expect, unlike those disappointing establishments around our coast which proclaim themselves to be 'Grand', 'Imperial', or having a 'Marine View', when they are, or have, no such thing. Built circa 1740, its architect decided to favour function over comfort. Beds were out. Benches—too much like beds. Chairs—merely a poor man's bench, and so discarded at the planning stage. Nonetheless, the complete absence of clutter of any kind gave the cell a wonderful sense of space, which ordinarily would have done two bachelors, exhausted after sampling the myriad wonders of Maidenhead, very well indeed for an overnight stay. Unfortunately, on the night we chose to stay there had been a regrettable lapse of organization, and several party-bookings must have been made simultaneously.

We could not see all the other guests in our room, but of those I could I counted thirty-two. Harris, with his slight advantage of height over me, claimed to see forty-seven. However many of us there were in total, the press of bodies kept us all upright, so the lack of furniture was not the problem it might otherwise have been.

Organization is definitely not the station's forte. They had evidently arranged for the entire staff to take the same night off, so that room service was non-existent. Moreover, the single, small bucket provided for the usual offices soon proved inadequate to the needs of so many guests; but for the sake of my more sensitive readers I shall say no more on that score.

Our fellow-guests were, like us, all young men dressed in boating blazers, a few even managing to have retained their straw boaters this far into the proceedings. All bore upon their faces and knuckles the traces of one or more contretemps during the night, and the malty odour of beer and whisky ran the eviller smells of that cell a creditably close race. Spirits were nonetheless still high, and some of the disagreements of the earlier evening had still not been settled to universal satisfaction.

'Mabel is mine, I tell you. And you keep your filthy paws off her.'

'If I see you so much as look at Rachel again, I swear I'll hang for you.'

And so the gentle conversation rumbled on. Fortunately, there was no violence: no-one could take a swing at the lothario next to him because of the crush of bodies. The gathering, therefore, had all the outward appearance of a popular, if male-only, after-river party, which belied the inward reality of a frustrated and bad-tempered mob.

In our corner we had the misfortune to be jambed up against our old friends Charles and Edgar. They had evidently fallen out.

'Emily is mine, I tell you. And you keep your filthy paws off her.'

'If I see you so much as look at Ethel again, I swear I'll hang for you.'

The antiphonal exchange was quite soothing, and reminded me of the times I have enjoyed the service of evening prayer in some quiet church on the river. Outside, the swallows swoop and climb, and the blackbird joins his sweet voice to ours. The low, bright sun fills the chancel with golden light, and all life renders praise to the Great Giver of Life. There are some that tell us that nature is red in tooth and claw. And she is. But they miss those occasions—which when they come are the more precious for being rare—when our Mother, Nature, says to us: 'Children, now put away your weapons, sheathe your claws. Declare a truce awhile, and learn from me the deeper lesson of life. Know that the fundamental truth of our Creator's will is—harmony.'

'Oh. So it's you again, is it?' Charles had recognized me and had, having bored of sparring with Edgar, set his sights on a new target. 'Rough up any more wounded old soldiers recently? Perhaps you have moved on to tougher opponents. See if you can go three rounds with a governess or a nursemaid, eh?'

'I wouldn't start, old boy. Not if I were you,' cut in Harris. 'The last man who offered violence to my friend here is now dead. And that was less than two hours ago.'

'Dead?' asked Charles, now considerably deflated. 'How?'

'You wouldn't believe me if I told you. My friend is highly trained and very resourceful, and can turn whatever comes to his hand into a deadly weapon. A trick he learned during his time at university in Germany, with the notorious Hamburgerverein, of which you have no doubt heard. Indeed, who has not?'

'Indeed,' said Charles, his confidence ebbing further.

'Let's just say that the coroner's verdict will read "Death by otter", and leave it at that, shall we?'

'"Death by otter"?' asked Charles blankly, drawing no doubt on all his medical knowledge to consider the myriad ways—none of them pleasant—by which this could occur. Then he looked me up and down, searching for any item which, in the hands of an expert, might be lethal. He caught sight of the straw boater I carried. He swallowed hard, and the colour drained from his face. After a pause, he addressed me.

'Look, old chap, I can see now that I was a bit hasty back at the pub. I'm sure you had your reasons for doing what you did. It's all otter—it's all water—under the bridge now. Let bygones be bygones, eh? That's my motter—er, motto.'

Before I could reply, there was a jangle of keys in the lock and the duty sergeant called out our names while three constables held back the press of bodies from the cell door. We were led back into the interrogation room where we had previously been questioned. Statements had been prepared for us to sign. They contained the same names we had been asked about again and again: the agent of a foreign power known only as 'Jan'; Miss Irene Adler, also known as 'The Woman', also known as Mrs Godfrey Norton; Mr Godfrey Norton; the King of Bohemia. And it contained our most solemn disavowals that any of these persons or names meant anything to us.

I was relieved to see that Harris's sole confession under questioning had been struck from the official record, namely that he 'was sure he had visited the King of Bohemia down Putney way once, and that J. had definitely been with me. Or was it the King William IV? Or perhaps it was the Rose and Crown after all?'

We were happy to sign.

When the forms were returned to the superintendent and he had checked our signatures to his satisfaction, he motioned to a constable who opened the door. A distinguished-looking gentleman of a professional mien and a vaguely military bearing entered and spoke.

'Yes, superintendent. These are the men!'

*   *   *

I flatter myself that, in the hands of a lesser writer, the arrival of Dr John H. Watson upon the scene of our incarceration could have been played for sheer melodrama. But it is my task merely to relate the facts, and let the reader supply the colour. The reader must imagine, from my bare testimony, both the depths of the despair to which our plight had brought us, and the ecstatic heights of relief that the good doctor's intervention occasioned. The reader must picture the pallor and helplessness that darkened our countenances as we stood in our cell, and then the smiles that wreathed our faces as we greeted our familiar neighbour and wept—yea, wept!—hot tears of joy upon his collar. But of such emotions I myself, the mere messenger of stern Fact alone, must needs be silent.

'Good evening, Dr Watson, you are most welcome,' said the superintendent. 'Is it true that you know these men and can vouch for their bona fides?'

'I do know them, superintendent. They are in effect both neighbours of mine. Jerome here rents the rooms above my friend Holmes's set. Harris here, and their friend Wingrave, spend most of their leisure hours with Jerome. They have a dog too, who rejoices in the name of Montmorency. Wingrave is a banker, Harris a legal man, and Jerome is between jobs, pretending to be a writer. They are all three harmless, and under the circumstances I am sure they will forgive me for saying that in my professional opinion they are all too feeble-minded to have taken any culpable part in the delicate matters now afoot.'

Harris and I stood open-mouthed. We had hardly exchanged so much as a 'Good evening' with Watson as we passed on the stair. And yet he had deduced, from such fleeting encounters alone, so much about us. Had Watson been knocking around in the Middle Ages, he would certainly have been burnt at the stake for sorcery.

Then the good doctor withdrew from his breast pocket a letter, and addressed the superintendent once more.

'In addition to my own testimony (which I hope is not negligible), I have written proof of these men's collective innocence. It is a letter addressed to them from the aforementioned George Wingrave, which arrived at Maidenhead post office by the evening post from London. It reads as follows:

"Dear Harris and J.,

It's a bit awkward back here, I'm afraid. Today I punched a clergyman and burnt down someone's house. But the bad news is Briony. She doesn't exist! At least, she does exist, but as a building, not a person. It's all a bit confusing, and I'm not sure I completely understand it all, but 'Briony Lodge' turns out to be a villa in Serpentine Avenue. It's the one I set fire to, but it was an accident and I did raise the alarm. So who was the Briony Lodge who came to see us, then? She seemed genuine enough, from what I remember. And what about those two German brutes who came looking for her? They were real enough. Well, they weren't real, they were imposters. But at least they were flesh and blood, not brick and tile like Briony. I think you should both come home at once and see what you can make of it. Gosh, this is more confusing than a Gilbert and Sullivan, isn't it?

I hope you are both well. I am quite well.

Mrs H. and Montmorency send their regards. The weather here is fine. How is it there?

Yours affectionately,

George."

Knowing that the police are not empowered to open private correspondence, I took it upon myself to open it, thinking that it might shed light upon what these men were doing here. I think, Superintendent, that it does: it shows them to be absolutely ignorant of all the relevant facts. I also hope, gentlemen, that in view of the generally corroborative nature of this letter with regard to your innocence, you will not press charges against me for this intrusion.'

'Not at all,' we said in unison.

Chapter Sixteen

The unaccountable rudeness of a mother and her offspring—The train lavatory not a dressing room

---

Friday 14 June

THE next morning we boarded the first train to town. Our compartment was shared with a mother and her two young sons. A few minutes after the train left Maidenhead, the mother went over to the window between us and lowered it with such force that we feared it might shatter in its frame. We also noticed that there was a grimace upon her face that had not been there when we first entered the compartment. However, the grimace was evidently a congenital condition, for I now noticed it upon her sons as well. A few minutes later, the mother stood again, gathered up her children and luggage, muttered something about the sort of people allowed to travel on the railways nowadays, and stormed out of the compartment. We were puzzled by this behaviour.

'Upset the lady, J.?' asked Harris, his eyes shut against the morning sun and his legs stretched out.

'Never so much as spoke a dickie bird. You?'

'No. Didn't seem to take to us, though, did she?'

'The boys were a bit put out too.'

'Strange that. Still, can't expect to conquer hearts wherever we go, can we? Each to his taste, and all that.'

'S'pose,' I replied, just before we both drifted off into a blissful sleep.

We were nearing Paddington when we both awoke, and realized from the awful smell that pervaded the compartment that we were wearing the same gear in which we had spent half the night in the holding cell. The odiferousness of our clothing had insured for us an empty compartment for the whole journey, but we had no wish to be detained for vagrancy upon our arrival in the Metropolis.

It is extraordinarily difficult to get dressed in the lavatory of a moving train, especially when time is against you. There is not enough space to hang the clothes you wish to get into, or to remove the clothes you wish to get out of. An item placed in an apparently secure location will be thrust without warning upon the floor, or in the basin, or worse. The movement of the train itself, which seems so regular and predictable when one is safely seated, suddenly becomes irregular and violent. You put your leg to a pair of trousers and you are thrown against a wall. You put your arm in a sleeve and the movement of the train dashes you against the towel rail, and you cut your head. There is not enough light to see by, even in broad daylight, and the mirror provided reflects only the smallest part of one's face, and one has no idea of the overall effect of one's new ensemble until you leave the lavatory compartment. Then young ladies faint while older ones go to fetch the guard.

It is as if the train lavatory has had enough and, like Spartacus of old, is in high revolt. I am of a proud and noble race, it seems to proclaim. I have a function, but the public abuses it. I shall teach them therefore that they may not oppress me any longer. If they wish to attend to their coiffeur or to shave, let them visit a barber's. Do they wish to change their clothes? Let them do so at home, and not be so fickle as to alter their dress during the day. If they try to do so against my stern command, then let them emerge from my gloomy portals with cut heads, nicked faces, dishevelled hair, and clothes awry. I have had enough of being used as a convenience.

It was a good thing I had brought so many clothes with me on this trip, as I may have remarked once or twice to Harris. Going up river, even by train, is a rum thing: you never know what to expect.

*   *   *

In the cab home I fell into a brown study. Miss Lodge's effect upon me had been far deeper than I had realized. By an irony of fate, the letter from George that had secured us freedom from a police charge had, in the same instant, revealed my dear Briony's complicity in the crime. What motive she may have had in spinning her false tale I could not tell, unless she meant to distract the real Holmes from the real Briony Lodge, and whatever intrigue there was about that place that involved kings and contraltos.

And yet, and yet… There was something about Briony that still rang true through all the falsity. Was it her precise, forthright manner that suggested she always spoke plainly and honestly? Whether she were addressing the girls in her charge (if she had any), or the very mightiest in the land, or St Peter himself at the Last Trump—it would make no difference to that noble heart. No, there was not an ounce of guile in her. Or were my thoughts simply those of a lovesick man, who judges character by the curve of a neck and gives credence to the prettiness of a mouth? I did not know. Of one thing only I was certain: that I would never see her again.

We paid off the cabbie, and went up to my rooms, giving Boots sixpence to bring up the luggage.

'Sixpence, guv?' replied Boots. 'Sixpence? Sixpence—to cover a lifetime's hosteopathy treatment and provide for my loved ones?'

I gave him another threepenny bit and he suddenly seemed quite contented. Boots will never be a businessman.

'Psst! Psst! This way, Mr J.!'

It was Mrs Hudson, waylaying us before we had reached my rooms.

'Whatever is it, Mrs H.?' I said.

'It's Miss Briony, sir. She's here in the house. I've hid her. Those two Germans were back here looking for her. Then she herself come along in the middle of the night, looking like a drownded rat, the poor lamb. She'd been hiding from them and thought they wouldn't come back here again, but I'm not so sure. I've got to go out now, sir. Mr Holmes is due back any minute and I've no porter for him. He loves 'is porter, he does, after a night out. Can get all mopey without it, and you know what that means. So can I leave her in your care?'

I nodded, hardly daring to believe this turn of events. Hardly daring even to breathe.

'That's very kind, Mr J. She's been looking forward to seeing you again, she has!'

Mrs Hudson led us into the kitchen, where Briony, looking lovelier than ever, was holding Montmorency to her bosom. For a moment, with the light streaming in from the pantry window and illuminating her hair, I dared to imagine... no, I can hardly admit it. And yet I must. If this small memoir of mine is to have any lasting worth, it must record the whole truth. I dared to imagine that one day that vision of loveliness would be holding not my dog but... I must write the words... our child!

'Miss Lodge! But I thought... George wrote and told us...'

'I know what you must think of me, but I can explain everything.'

'We cannot stay here,' I pointed out. We must go to my rooms. We can keep you safe there. Come on, Harris. Harris?'

'With you in a sec, old chap. Do you know how long it's been since breakfast? And I see that Mrs Hudson has just made another of her superb fruit pies.'

'All right, then. But don't dally, and come up as soon as you are finished. We must protect Miss Lodge.'

'Righto,' said Harris, spoon already in hand.

*   *   *

I let Briony and Montmorency into my room and was careful to lock the door behind us. It was an irregular way of entertaining a young lady, but I felt I had Mrs H's blessing.

'Mr Jerome. J.—I may call you J., mayn't I? It is not too familiar of me, is it? I know from Mrs Hudson what Mr Wingrave has told you about me, for he also told it to her: that I am an imposter. I can only say it is not true. My name is Briony Lodge and I can prove it if necessary. Until yesterday I did not even know that in the same avenue as mine there was also a house called 'Briony Lodge'. It is at the other end of the avenue, and in my brief time here, and with my work and late hours at the school, I had no cause to explore up there. When I first heard, I assumed that the letters I had received were intended for the house; that someone there was being threatened and not me after all. But that does not explain it, does it?'

'Why not?' I asked, secretly joying within myself to hear this magnificent girl affirm her innocence.

'Don't you remember? The letters were addressed very specifically to "The Woman Briony Lodge"— don't you see? The woman, and not the villa! They were meant for me! But why and how, that I do not understand.'

At this point there was a knock on the door—Harris back from his demolition of Mrs Hudson's latest creation, no doubt—and I walked over to unlock the door for him. Eagerly I resumed my conversation with Briony.

'No, Miss Lodge. You are quite wrong. I am sorry to be direct, but I must be on this point, as you would be with your girls if any of them were to make a mistake in punctuation.' I delighted to see her reaction.

'Punctuation, J.? I do not understand.'

'Check your envelopes, the ones you showed me. You will find that they were addressed not to "The Woman Briony Lodge" but rather to "The Woman, Briony Lodge". The postman knew of two Briony Lodges in Serpentine Avenue, as it was his job to know, and assumed that the designation was to help him. What he did not know was that the resident of Briony Lodge, Irene Adler, had an alias, as I heard last night from the superintendent of Maidenhead Police, which her agents used: "The Woman". The letters were intended for her after all. You have nothing whatever to do with this conspiracy. Your innocence is assured!'

I took Briony's hands in mine, and stared into those twin pools of blue.

From the open door came the sound of a slow handclap. If ever a handclap could be described as dripping in sarcasm, it would have been that one.

'Don't be an ass, Harris,' I said, without looking away from those mesmerizing eyes.

'Not at all, Mr Jerome,' said a voice that was not Harris's. 'You have done very well for an amateur. Very well indeed. Under other circumstances I could happily have found a man of your skills a place in my organization. But, alas, quite another fate lies in store for you: you know too much. May I come in? Thank you.'

Now I did turn around, to see the man who had called himself Lestrade close the door to and stride to the centre of the room. He took out a Mauser pistol from one pocket of his raincoat and a silencer from the other, and fitted them together with a practised air.

'Oh, do not try to call for your friend Mr Harris. You would in any case be dead before he got here. Besides, my assistant Steiner is with him in the kitchen. Steiner does not say much, but he gets his point across, if you know what I mean. There is no-one else in the house at all. No-one to disturb us. You know, it grieves me to have dispose of such a lovely young couple as you—to say nothing of the dog, of course—on such a short acquaintance. But, as you can imagine, it goes with the job, as your quaint English phrase has it.'

At this, Montmorency began to whine pitifully and to pull me back by the trouser leg. Briony edged back with us, until we reached the wall and could retreat no further.

'You are forgetting one thing, Lestrade. If that is your name,' I said.

'Indeed? I cannot imagine I have done so. And, if I have, would it not be extremely foolish of you to remind me of it at this juncture?'

'Mrs Hudson told us that Holmes was expected back at any moment. He is bound to notice that something is wrong, and your game will be up.'

'You are of course quite right, Mr Jerome. (Oh, by the way, my name is Bahn. Otto Bahn, not Lestrade. I believe that you have a strange habit in this country of being allowed to know the name of your executioner.) There was always the chance of Mr Holmes coming back. But I have it on excellent authority that he is not. Not yet at least.'

'How do you know?' asked Briony, her voice clear and unafraid.

'Because I happen to know a peculiarity of your little dog. If anyone comes to the street door, he puts his paws on the window sill and barks. (This information cost me just the price of a pint of porter with your excellent Boots—whose actual name is Williams, by the way, not that I expect the English bourgeoisie like yourselves to take an interest in your lower-classes.) Even if Holmes were to return now, your dog would warn me in sufficient time to kill you both and leave by the servants' staircase.

'Good—I see that you have lined yourselves up against the wall in the time-honoured fashion, without any bidding from me. Now, if both of you would keep very still, I can assure you a quick death without suffering. I am an excellent shot and can do this with two rounds only. I do not intend to waste a bullet on your little dog. My boots are quite heavy enough, don't you think?'

I took Briony's hand in mine and squeezed it. She squeezed back, but continued to gaze ahead with those intense blue eyes, defying her murderer to the last. She showed no fear whatever. Montmorency rubbed against the back of our calves, whimpering softly.

Bahn raised the Mauser and took aim at my forehead.

Two shots rang out in quick succession. And Otto Bahn fell forward, lifelessly, to the floor.

Chapter Seventeen

*The real Inspector Lestrade—A dreadful
conspiracy unveiled—How George saved the
day without ever understanding anything*

THERE were six of us: Briony Lodge, William
Samuel Harris, George Wingrave, Montmorency,
myself—and Inspector Lestrade. The real one, I mean.
Not Otto Bahn, who called himself Lestrade, whose
body was even now being removed from the house in
a police ambulance. We sat in the kitchen, each one
of us with a cup of strong, sweet tea, with just a spot
in it of the stuff that both cheers and inebriates. A
sovereign remedy for shock, says Mrs Hudson. And
who were we to disagree?

'Well, gentlemen—and you, miss—it seems you
are all to be congratulated,' said Lestrade expansively.
'Miss Lodge and Mr J. managed to disarm, and to kill
with his own gun, one of the most desperate foreign
agents operating in London. And you, Mr Harris,
laid his lieutenant out cold with a piece of kitchen

equipment. But *how* you all did it… that's what I want to know!'

'The greedy blighter had eaten Mrs Hudson's fruit pie and still wanted more. I told him I thought she had baked some Welsh cakes as well, and suggested he took a look in the stove. He never expected the girdle stone!'

'And now you must tell us something, Inspector,' said Briony, deftly changing the subject. 'What was the mystery of Serpentine Avenue? I have heard all sorts of things about mysterious contraltos and crowned heads. What was it all about, and where did I fit into their scheme?'

'Well, I suppose you have a right to know,' said Lestrade, scratching his head. 'But first I shall have to swear you to complete secrecy on your word of honour as a gentleman or as a lady, depending. It seems that the King of Bohemia had once known this Irene Adler person very well, if you get my drift (begging your pardon for speaking direct, miss), and there existed a rather compromising photograph of the pair. The King was due to be married to another party, and was naturally anxious to retrieve the said item in case it were held over his head for blackmail. But Miss Adler was equally anxious to hold on to it. It was her security, if you like. He sent his best agents after it, but Miss Adler outwitted them every time.'

'She sounds like a formidable woman,' said Briony.

'Oh, she is that, miss. I think you two would get on if ever you met... Anyway, at last the King saw sense, and engaged the services of Mr Holmes, like he should have done in the first place. And there you might have thought it was all over bar the shouting, as they say. But what neither the King nor Miss Adler knew was that there was a group of Bohemian anarchists loose in England. They wanted the photograph in order to embarrass the King and start an anarchist revolution over there. They got spooked good and proper when Mr Holmes joined the fun. So they started sending orange pips to Miss Adler—a familiar enough way among these secret societies of threatening imminent assassination—to panic her into making the photograph public.'

'It wasn't familiar to me,' protested George, sounding rather aggrieved. 'I mean, that business of the orange pips.'

'Nor to me,' I said.

'Well, sirs, that just goes to show you don't move in the wrong circles. Now these anarchists might have pulled it off too, but for two factors they could not have predicted. The first was that Mr Holmes's brother, who I understand is quite a big-wig in Whitehall, knew all about them and Dr

Watson was sent to their hide-out in Oxford to keep an eye on them, supported by the local police. The second factor was that, unfortunately for them, the orange pips got sent to Miss Lodge by mistake. Miss Lodge came to Baker Street, and they feared that Mr Holmes would put two and two together. But by a stroke of luck—for them, this time—Miss Lodge was sent up to 221d instead of 221b. Mr Harris and Mr J. go off to Maidenhead, and in some manner I'm still not clear about, did for the anarchist called 'Jan', then came back here, and accounted for Bahn in the same way and put Steiner in the prison hospital. That's what I call a result.'

'And let's not forget Miss Lodge's contribution,' I said firmly, and Montmorency seemed to bark his approval, to general mirth.

'No, Mr J.—a braver woman than Miss Lodge I have not yet met,' said Lestrade.

'And let's not forget George,' said Harris, sportingly. 'Without his letter J. and I would still be in that Maidenhead lock-up.'

'Mr Wingrave did more than that—much more—I assure you. You see, it had been Mr Holmes's plan all along to gain entry to Miss Adler's villa by posing as a clergyman who had been knocked down in a fracas outside her front door. He then hoped to observe where she hid the photographs by raising the alarm of fire. A woman, you see, will invariably rescue the thing most dear to her before making her own escape. For a mother, it would be a babe in arms. For an adventuress like Irene Adler, it would be her assets. Mr Wingrave not only laid Mr Holmes out—incidentally, Mr Wingrave, Mr Holmes asked me to tell you to feint with your right before striking with your left, and of course to work on your accuracy—but even set fire to the curtains which had the desired effect on Miss Adler's psychology, as Mr Holmes was able to observe from the comfort of his sofa. So—a fine job all round. If ever I find myself stretched and in need of cool brains and stout fists, I might well call on you again, if I may.'

Lestrade pushed his cup and saucer aside and stood.

'And now, if you'll excuse me, I have to get back to the Yard. You would not believe the paperwork this case has generated. Why, even the message on that little wrapper thing that Jan the anarchist dropped…'

'Die Hamburgerischeschokoladevereins-gesellschaft?' offered Harris.

'That's the one. Did you know that that string of letters contains thirty-two possible combinations of secret messages, if the target language is English, according to the lab boys? Six hundred and forty-eight, if it is Welsh. I reckon it was just a chocolate wrapper, though. Anyway, good afternoon, Miss. Gents. I know my way out.'

As Lestrade left the kitchen, Mrs Hudson entered.

'Oh, Mr J. That German friend of yours has left a terrible mess on your carpet. Right in the middle of the room as well. I'll do my best to get it up, but there'll always be a stain. I've a good mind to stop it out of your deposit.'

'Do as you wish, Mrs H. I really don't mind,' I laughed, looking deep into Briony's eyes.

'Well, there is an old round rug I never use which would cover up the bloodstain nicely. No-one would ever know. Now then, gentlemen, if you would kindly leave my kitchen I would much appreciate it. I have plenty to be getting on with, and what with inanimate Germans cluttering up the place I am all behind. Oh, not you, Briony, nor you, Mr J. I think you two need to go into my parlour and have a quiet word, don't you? And Montmorency, of course.'

Chapter Eighteen

The mysteries of canine communication—
My proposal to Miss Lodge—Her surprising
proposition to me—Man proposes, Dog disposes

WITHOUT any demur, Briony, Montmorency, and I went into Mrs H.'s private parlour, conscious that we had been granted an exceptional honour.

'Well, Miss Lodge,' I said when we were seated.

'Well, Mr Jerome,' she replied.

Then we both fell about laughing.

'We shouldn't really laugh, you know. The man is dead,' I reproved her, but was unable to keep a straight face myself.

'I know,' she said, still laughing heartily. 'I suppose it is just the sudden release of pent-up emotion. It's not in the least funny. He couldn't have had any idea what was happening when Mr Holmes fired those shots through the floor. And all because Mrs Hudson hadn't got him his porter in time!'

Then she collapsed into renewed peals of laughter.

'But… but what I don't understand is why Montmorency did not bark. He must have heard Holmes enter by the street door.'

'Oh, J.—you really don't speak Montmorency at all, do you? Monty only barks when a *stranger* comes to the street door. Mr Holmes isn't a stranger. He lives here. But one always *expects* a dog to bark. That is where Lestrade—I mean Otto Bahn—made his mistake. Monty was the dog that did not bark.'

Montmorency—or 'Monty', as he had now been christened by Briony, and I admit the name does suit him very well—shared himself between us, jumping and wagging his tail before quietly settling down on Briony's lap with a highly proprietorial air. Our laughter had subsided, and I was alone in the parlour with the two beings whose company I craved most. George and Harris were good friends—the best—but Briony and Montmorency were like a part of myself. There was something I knew I had to ask Briony. But I did not know if it were the right time.

'Miss Lodge—Briony—I once asked you if there were anyone with whom you had an understanding of any sort. I must confess that I had another motive in asking you that question.'

'I thought you might have had, J.'

'Briony, you have come into my life and turned everything in it upside down. Or rather, you have turned it the right way up. You have even re-named my dog—though I have to say he does seem to like it.'

'He's always been "Monty", J. He told me the first time I met him.'

'Briony, you are the cleverest, the bravest, and the most beautiful woman I have ever met. I know it is far too soon. But I also know that if I do not ask you I shall regret it all my days. You have changed one name today. Is it too much to hope that you would consider changing another—your own?'

'I really don't think "Monty" would suit me, J. Besides, just think of the confusion that would arise.'

'No, I mean…'

'I'm sorry, J., I should not jest about something that means so much to you. I was not unaware of your feelings for me, and your question, flattering as it is, of course, was not wholly unexpected. I say this not out of arrogance, but as a simple matter of fact. It is the lot of every woman to be proposed to several times, sometimes several times the same day. Young men are very free with proposals, and don't always mean what they say, or say what they mean. Often they do not mean it at all, and are simply practising for the day when they will.'

'Briony, I am quite earnest…'

'Then you must recognize that I also am earnest when I say that I have resolved never to marry. I told you once before that I am devoted to teaching, and I have never yet spoken an untruth.'

'But is there no chance you may not reconsider? I spoke too boldly, and too soon. Perhaps in a few months, a year from now, I might again…'

'No. It would be cruel indeed of me to offer false hope to one who is so very dear. Once resolved upon a course, I never waver from it. Let us be friends, J., the best of friends. Friendships between the sexes are too rare, and should be cultivated. It is nearly the twentieth century, after all.'

'If that is as much as you feel you can be to me,' I replied, almost trembling with emotion, 'then it is more than I could ever want.'

My mouth suddenly felt very dry, and my eyes unusually damp.

'You are a true friend, J., and much more than a friend: for I owe my life to you.'

Now she took my hands in hers, and stared intently into my eyes.

'J., you have been open and frank with me. May I be as open and as frank with you?'

'Of course, Briony.'

'When I say that I intend never to marry, that does not mean that I wish to be entirely alone. The teaching profession is a lonely one, I have found. The girls take up so much of one's time, energy, and emotions that one cannot easily cultivate adult friendships.'

'What of your fellow mistresses? Are they not sympathetic?'

'They are wonderful people, J. But none of them, I think, could ever be a true soul-mate to me. Indeed, until I met you I did not think such a thing possible. Since meeting you, J., I have realized that I have needs, the needs of a young woman for companionship, for laughter, for…'

She paused, and lowered her gaze to the floor.

'… for the physical dimension of friendship.' My mouth became even drier.

Still unable to look at me directly, Briony continued.

'J., I have a proposition of my own to make. I could not even utter it—I could not even think it—if I did not trust you absolutely and regard you as my truest and dearest friend upon this globe. I wish to propose an arrangement between us. It is not a conventional one. To some it will seem scandalous, Bohemian even. Indeed, I realize that my very suggesting it may shock your noble, upright soul to the core, and end our young friendship on the spot.'

My mouth was now very dry indeed.

'Speak, my darling,' I said, hardly believing what she was saying, even if it was nearly the twentieth century. 'Do not fear, my beloved. Do not be afraid of expressing your heart's desires.'

'You promise you will not be shocked?'

'I promise, my darling. I will not.'

It was, in the words of the excellent Lestrade, a definite result.

She looked up wordlessly, her blue eyes, flecked with indigo, so large. I wished to drown in them.

'Then let Monty move in with me.'

I pulled away from her so suddenly that her hands fell back into her lap.

'What!' I said.

'What's the matter, J.? Did you not realize that is what I meant? What else could you think I... '

'Of course,' I intervened hurriedly. 'Yes. I knew that is what you were asking. Naturally. What else could it have been? Ha! Ha! It's just that Montmorency and I... well, we are soul-mates too.'

'What nonsense, J.! That Monty is fond of you and you of him, I shall always allow. That you are soul-friends, never. Why, you hardly understand a word he says.'

It was true, I reflected, that Montmorency was sometimes less eloquent than I would have liked. But I had always put that down to his being a dog.

'Let us strike a deal,' Briony said suddenly. 'Let Monty himself decide between us, and let his decision be final.'

'Very well,' I said. 'Let Montmorency decide.' (The name Monty really did not suit him after all). I still felt that Briony had not quite grasped the point that Montmorency was my dog, not a disputed enclave in the Balkans. However, it seemed a just solution.

'Monty: do you want to live here with Uncle Jerome, or come to live with me in my house?'

Montmorency looked first at Briony, and then turned to look at me. He cocked his head to the side in the way that he always did, then came and brushed against my leg. It was, however, merely the fox-terrier way of saying good-bye, for he then gave a whimper of delight, ran over to Briony and sprang on to her lap. He stared up into those indigo-blue eyes for a long time. She stared back.

I was thoroughly confused. Of whom was I more jealous—Monty for stealing the heart of my beloved, or Briony for taking my dog? At the heart of every man on this planet there is, I believe, a core of Dog. It is the Dog in us that makes us Men. How could it be otherwise? When womenkind captivate us, and our eyes bulge, and our tongues loll, and we leap and dance at their whim, and roll over upon our backs, is it not merely the Eternal Canine responding to the Eternal Feminine?

Briony would take no man into her service; but by taking my dog, Montmorency, I feel that in some ineffable way our three souls were entwined.

And, for me, that would always be the real Mystery of Briony Lodge.

*   *   *

And so, dear reader, my tale is complete, and our time together has come to an end. If ever we meet in the flesh, it would be my pleasure to let you buy me a drink. (May I recommend the Mitre on the Marylebone Road? You can get a chop and two glasses of Bass for 1/6d, and it would still be cheap at twice the price.) We can yarn about your adventures and mine—for yes, I still have a few more to tell if time and paper allow—until the embers die in the fire and the landlord gets shirty and tells us he has a bed to go to even if we don't. Let our conversation range far and wide, but one limitation alone I insist upon, and if you have read this story to its end you will not ask the reason for it. That one thing is:

to say *nothing* of the dog.

Acknowledgements

My first debt is, naturally, to anyone who has handed over their hard-earned cash to buy this book: thank you. I also wish to thank Dr Sarah Walton for her enthusiastic support, and for teaching me so much when the arrangement was supposed to be the other way round. I am also indebted to Professor Martin Goodman and to the Barbican Press. My admiration for the writings of JKJ and ACD, which will I hope be obvious, is fully shared by my companion on 'the River of Life', to whom it is a pleasure to dedicate this lucubration.